Welcome to t[...]
Presents!

This month read the final installment of Lynne Graham's trilogy VIRGIN BRIDES, ARROGANT HUSBANDS, *The Spanish Billionaire's Pregnant Wife.* Leandro Marquez ruthlessly stops at nothing to wed Molly when he discovers she's pregnant with his child! And don't miss the first part of our fabulous new series INTERNATIONAL BILLIONAIRES, which starts when shy, hardworking Holly is swept off her feet by the magnificent Prince Casper in Sarah Morgan's *The Prince's Waitress Wife.* Expect emotions to reach fever pitch in Carole Mortimer's *The Mediterranean Millionaire's Reluctant Mistress* when tycoon Alejandro is determined to claim his secret baby and possess Brynne in the process. And will an innocent plain Jane convince Sheikh Tair Al Sharif to let go of his mistrustful nature in Kim Lawrence's *Desert Prince, Defiant Virgin?* Business tycoon Santos Cordero is intent on seducing Alexa into a marriage of convenience in Kate Walker's *Cordero's Forced Bride,* while sexual tension heightens when Stefano seeks revenge after being left at the altar in Kate Hewitt's *The Italian's Bought Bride.* Be prepared for a battle of the sexes in Robyn Grady's *Confessions of a Millionaire's Mistress* as Celeste and Ben find they want the same thing in the bedroom...but different things from life! Plus, look out for Nicola Marsh's *The Boss's Bedroom Agenda,* in which a sizzling night spent together between Beth and her gorgeous new boss, Aidan, changes everything!

We'd love to hear what you think about Harlequin Presents. E-mail us at Presents@hmb.co.uk, or join in the discussions at www.iheartpresents.com and www.sensationalromance.blogspot.com, where you'll also find more information about books and authors!

Surrender To The Sheikh

He's proud, passionate, primal—
dare she surrender to the Sheikh?

Feel warm winds blowing through your hair
and the hot desert sun on your skin
as you are transported to exotic lands....
As the temperature rises, let yourself be
seduced by our sexy, irresistible sheikhs.

If you love our men of the desert,
look for more stories in this
enthralling miniseries, coming soon.

Available only from Harlequin Presents®.

Kim Lawrence

DESERT PRINCE, DEFIANT VIRGIN

Surrender To
The Sheikh

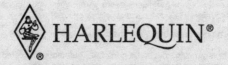

HARLEQUIN®

TORONTO • NEW YORK • LONDON
AMSTERDAM • PARIS • SYDNEY • HAMBURG
STOCKHOLM • ATHENS • TOKYO • MILAN • MADRID
PRAGUE • WARSAW • BUDAPEST • AUCKLAND

Recycling programs
for this product may
not exist in your area.

ISBN-13: 978-0-373-12796-2
ISBN-10:   0-373-12796-0

DESERT PRINCE, DEFIANT VIRGIN

First North American Publication 2009.

Copyright © 2008 by Kim Lawrence.

www.eHarlequin.com

Printed in U.S.A.

Printed in U.S.A.

CHAPTER ONE

PEOPLE assumed that Tair Al Sharif was a natural diplomat, but they were wrong.

He was so *not* a diplomat—though there had been many occasions when that role had been forced upon him by necessity—that as his cousin's glance once more drifted from him to the young Englishwoman seated on the opposite side of the table he wanted quite badly to drag the other man from his chair, give him a good shake and demand to know what the hell he thought he was playing at.

'How is your father, Tair?'

The soft buzz of conversation around the table stilled as Tair removed his steely stare from the Crown prince of Zarhat's profile and turned his attention to the man who was the hereditary ruler of that country.

'Hassan's death was a shock to him.'

The king sighed and shook his head. 'A man should not outlive his children. It is not the natural order of things. Still he has you, Tair, and that must be a comfort to him.'

If this was the case his father was hiding it well.

There was an ironic glitter in Tair's blue eyes as his thoughts were drawn back to his last verbal exchange with his father.

'I trusted you and what did you do, Tair?' King Malik's face had been suffused with a dark colour as he'd slammed his fist down on the table, causing all the heavy silver to jump.

Years ago when he had been a boy, Tair had struggled to hide his reaction to his father's sometimes violent and unpredictable outbursts, though such displays of unbridled fury had left him sick to the stomach. Now he did not need to struggle, as his father's rages no longer seemed frightening to him, just vaguely distasteful.

'It is a pity it wasn't *you* who walked in front of that car instead of your brother. *He* knew what loyalty and respect is due me. *He* would have supported me in this, not taken advantage of my grief to go behind my back.'

'I tried to contact you in Paris.'

His father's grief had not interfered in any noticeable manner with his social life.

King Malik dismissed this comment with a wave of his short, heavily ringed fingers and a contemptuous snort.

'But I was told you were not to be disturbed.' Tair knew this had been shorthand for his father being in the middle of a very high-stakes poker game.

The king's eyes narrowed further as he glared at his remaining son without a hint of affection.

'Your problem, Tair, is you have no vision. You do not think on the grand scale, but of such things as a water-treatment plant…' His sneer registered utter contempt for such a project. 'You exchanged those mineral rights for a water-treatment plant instead of a new yacht!'

'Not just a water-treatment plant, but an undertaking to recruit locally whenever possible, a training programme for our people and fifty per cent of the profits for them once they have recouped a percentage of their initial outlay.'

The deal he had renegotiated had not made the international firm he was dealing with exactly happy. They had been under the impression he was there to rubber stamp the contract as it stood, but they had at least viewed him with grudging respect as they had walked away looking like men who were not quite sure what had just happened to them.

Of course, Tair conceded, he'd had the element of surprise on his side. Next time—though considering his father's reaction that might not be any time soon—he would not have that advantage.

But Tair was not a man to avoid challenges.

'Profits!' His father had dismissed those intangible projected figures with a snap of his swollen fingers. Over-indulgence had left its mark on his coarsened features and his once athletic body. 'And when will that be? I could have had the yacht next month.'

His suggestion that it would perhaps be no great hardship to make do with last year's yacht had not been received well! And though Tair had not expected, or fortunately needed, praise, the lecture had been hard to take.

It was much easier to accept the censorious finger his uncle waved in his direction because Tair knew that, unlike his own father, King Hakim's remonstrance was well intentioned. His uncle was a man who had always put the welfare of his people above his own comfort and would be able to appreciate what Tair was trying to achieve.

'Remember the next time you feel the urge to fly into a desert storm…*alone*…that you are all your father has left.'

It was hard to tell from his manner which action appalled his uncle the most: the danger of the desert storm or the fact his nephew had not travelled with an entourage of hundreds as befitted his station in life.

'There are responsibilities in being heir.'

Tair inclined his head in courteous acknowledgement of the royal rebuke. 'I am new to the role, Uncle, so I'm bound to make some errors.'

From the moment Tair had become heir to the throne many had considered his life public property and he accepted this, but there were some freedoms that he was not willing to relinquish. He needed places, moments and people with whom he could be himself in order to preserve his sanity.

'But you are not new to fobbing off old men. Do you think I don't know that you smile, say the right things and then do exactly what you want, Tair? However I know that, despite your action-man antics, you are aware of your duties. More aware than your brother ever was. I know one should not speak ill of the dead, but I say nothing now that I would not have said to his face and nothing I have not in the past said to your father.

'Malik did nobody any favours when he turned a blind eye to your brother's scandals and as for the dubious business dealings…?' Clicking his tongue, King Hakim shook his leonine head in disapproval. 'I have always been of the opinion that your country would have been better off if you had been born the elder.'

It wasn't often that Tair struggled for words, but, more accustomed to defending his actions from criticism, he was stunned to uncomfortable silence by this unexpected tribute from his uncle.

It was Beatrice who came to his rescue.

'I wouldn't mind getting my pilot's licence one day.'

The innocent comment from a heavily pregnant and glowing princess successfully diverted her father-in-law's attention from his nephew—as Tair was sure it was intended to—and began a good-natured joking debate among the younger generation around the table that centred on the hotly disputed superior ability of men to master any skill that required hand-eye co-ordination.

Everyone joined in except the mouselike English girl, who

either through shyness or total lack of social skills—Tair suspected the latter—had barely spoken a word throughout the meal unless directly addressed.

The second silent party was Tariq.

Tair's irritation escalated and his suspicion increased as he watched the pair through icy blue eyes.

Tariq was the man who had it all, including a wife who adored him, a wife who was carrying his first child.

Tair's expression softened as his glance flickered to the other end of the table where Beatrice Al Kamal sat looking every inch the regal princess even when she winked at him over the head of her father-in-law the king.

He turned his head, the half-smile that was tugging at his own lips fading as he saw that Tariq was still staring like some pathetic puppy at the English mouse.

Tair's lip curled in disgust. He had always liked and admired the other man, and had always considered his cousin strong not only in the physical but also in the moral sense. Tair had felt it couldn't have happened to a more deserving man when Tariq had met and married the glorious Titian-haired Beatrice after a whirlwind romance.

If two people were ever meant to be together it was Beatrice and Tariq. Their clear devotion had touched even Tair's cynical heart, and made him hope in his less realistic moments that there was such a soul mate waiting for him somewhere, though even if there was it seemed unlikely they were destined to be together.

His future was intrinsically linked with that of the country he would one day rule. What his country needed and deserved after years of neglect by his father and Hassan, who had both been of the opinion the country was their own personal bank, was political and financial stability. It was Tair's duty to make a marriage that supplied both. Improving transport links and dragging the medical facilities of Zabrania, the neighbouring country to Zarhat, into the twenty-first century were more important things than true love.

He directed another icy glare at his cousin, and considered the other man's stupidity. Tariq didn't seem to have a clue as to how lucky he was!

Didn't the man know he had it all?

And even if he wasn't insane enough to risk his marriage by actually being unfaithful—though in Tair's eyes the distinction between fantasy and physical infidelity was at best blurred—he was obviously stupid enough to risk hurting Beatrice by being so damned obvious.

Even a total imbecile could have picked up on the signals his cousin was being so mystifyingly indiscreet about hiding, and Beatrice was far from stupid.

It was totally inexplicable to Tair that Tariq could have so little respect for his wife that he would insult her this way, and for what…?

He allowed his own scornful gaze to drift in the direction of the English girl, who was clearly not the innocent she seemed because no man acted like Tariq without some encouragement. Tair tried and failed to see something in the mouselike girl that could tempt a man like Tariq…or for that matter any man!

Unlike red-headed, voluptuous Beatrice, this was not a girl who would turn heads. Small and slight, her brown hair secured in a twist at the nape of her neck—a good neck, Tair grudgingly noticed as he allowed his glance to linger momentarily on the slender pale column—she was not the sort of woman who exuded any strong allure for the opposite sex.

Trying to picture the small oval-shaped face without the large heavy-framed spectacles that were perched on the end of a slightly tip-tilted nose, Tair conceded that an investment in contact lenses might make her more than passable.

But such a change would not alter the fact that her body, covered at this moment in a peculiar sacklike dress the shade of mud, totally lacked the feminine curves which, like most men, he found attractive in the opposite sex.

His blue eyes narrowed as he watched the English girl turn her head to meet Tariq's eyes. For a moment the two simply looked at one another as though there were nobody else in the room. The outrage, locked in Tair's chest like a clenched fist, tightened another notch.

Then she smiled, her long curling eyelashes sweeping downwards creating a shadow across her smooth, softly flushed cheeks and the corners of her mouth. How had he missed the blatant sensuality of that full pouting lower lip?

Tair's mild concern and annoyance at his cousin's uncharacteristic behaviour morphed abruptly into genuine apprehension. Up until this point he had thought that his cousin had simply needed reminding that he was one of the good guys; now it seemed that more might be required.

This silent exchange suggested to him a worrying degree of intimacy. For the first time he seriously considered the possibility that this situation had progressed beyond mild flirtation.

Tair's long fingers tightened around the glass he was holding. Under the dark shield of his lashes his blue eyes, now turned navy with anger, slid around the table. The other guests at the family party continued to talk and laugh, seemingly oblivious to the silent communication between Tariq and the deceptively demure guest.

His brows twitched into a straight line above his strong masterful nose. Were they all blind?

How was it possible, he wondered incredulously, that he was the only person present who could see what was going on?

Could they not see the connection between these two?

Then his study of his guests revealed that Beatrice was also watching the interchange between her husband and friend. Tair's admiration of the woman his cousin had married went up another level when she responded to a comment made by her brother-in-law, Khalid, with a relaxed smile that hid whatever hurt or anxiety she might be feeling.

Beatrice was a classy lady. Clearly her mouse friend was not; she was a predator in mouse's clothing and his cousin was her prey.

He briefly considered the option of speaking directly to Tariq and telling him point-blank he was playing with fire. Such a discussion would end at best in harsh words and at worst in an exchange of blows—not really ideal from either a personal or political perspective. On reflection he decided it would be better by far to speak to the woman who was pursuing Tariq.

He would warn Miss Mouse that he would not stand by and watch her ruin the marriage of his friends. And if Miss Mouse didn't listen he would have to take direct action. He had no idea what form that direct action would take, but Tair's inspiration had so far not let him down. He had frequently walked into a room full of dignitaries whom his brother had insulted with no idea what he was going to say, but the right words had always come.

Though maybe this situation would require more than words… He gave a mental shrug, as he was capable of that too. Capable, according to some, of great ruthlessness, but Tair did not think of it in such emotive terms, he just did what was necessary and he never asked anyone else to perform an unpleasant task that he himself was not willing to do.

He looked at the sexy curve of the Mouse's mouth and wondered if that unpleasantness would take the form of sampling those lips…? Perhaps at a chosen moment when his actions could be observed by his cousin. The plan, unlike the

lady, had some virtue as he was sure Tariq was not a man who
would enjoy sharing any more than he would.

She was, he mused, staring at that mouth, nothing like any
woman he had ever kissed. She had nothing to recommend
her beyond neatness, a conniving nature and a sexy—actually
very sexy—mouth, and he had done worse to help a friend.

The Mouse, perhaps sensing his study, suddenly stopped
gazing at Tariq and turned her head, the action briefly causing
her gaze to collide with his cold, hostile stare.

He watched with clinical detachment, the guilty colour rise
up her slender neck until her small face was suffused with heat.

His lip curled in contempt as he smiled and watched her
literally recoil before she looked away. At least she now
knew that there was someone who was not fooled by her
meek and mild act.

Tariq was still wearing the dark formal suit that he had been
wearing at dinner, but his tie now hung loose around his neck.

Molly closed the door and motioned him to a chair. She
perched on the edge of the big canopied bed suspecting her
cotton pyjamas looked totally incongruous against the silken
opulence, much the same way as she looked totally incongruous and out of place in the palace.

Some of the awkwardness and wariness she felt in Tariq's
presence had dissipated over the past couple of weeks but she
still couldn't totally relax around him.

She got the impression that he too was still feeling his
way. Which wasn't that surprising given this relationship was
still very new for them both. Fortunately Khalid, with his
naturally outgoing nature, had not been similarly stilted and
Molly felt much more at ease in his company.

Tariq, tall and lean, took the chair, turned it round, then
straddled it, resting his hands on the back as he looked across

at her. Molly realised that Beatrice had not been exaggerating when she had told her that her husband was not a man who felt any need to fill silences. Molly, impatient to know the reason for his visit, stifled her impulse to demand an explanation.

'I have not disturbed you? You were not asleep?'

She shook her head and there was another lengthy silence while she wondered some more why he had come.

'Khalid is concerned he might have offended you.'

Molly's bewilderment was genuine. 'Why would he think that?'

'He introduced you to Tair as Beatrice's friend.' For once Tariq had not been pleased to see his cousin and he had been hard put not to show his lack of enthusiasm for the extra dinner guest. 'He is afraid,' he explained, 'that you might mistake his reasons for not revealing your true identity.'

Tariq's voice receded into the distance as an image rose in Molly's head of the tall man with the electric blue eyes who had arrived at dinner looking dusty but remarkably good considering he had apparently just made an emergency landing at the airport after flying through an unexpected dust storm.

'The families are connected, loads of intermarriage. He's a cousin and heir to the throne of Zabrania.' Beatrice had explained the stranger's presence in a quiet aside to Molly while the men spoke together in a bewildering mixture of rapid Arabic, French and English.

'He has blue eyes!' Deep cerulean blue, the most intense shade that Molly had ever seen.

'You noticed?'

Hard not to!

'Apparently blue eyes crop up every so often in the Al Sharif family. There's a nice story about that, according to family legend. How true it is, I don't know, but they say a Viking got lost way back when. Rumour has it he got a bit too friendly with a royal princess and since then the blue eyes pop up every few generations. Tair is quite a looker, isn't he?'

Vaguely aware of Beatrice's amusement but totally unable to control her own expression, Molly closed her mouth with an audible snap and lowered her gaze, wondering if it was the incredible level of testosterone circulating in the room that was responsible for her erratic heartbeat.

'Really…?' she said, adopting a look of wide-eyed, exaggerated innocence. 'I hadn't noticed.'

Her humour was a little shaky, though Beatrice seemed not to notice, responding to the husky irony with an appreciative chuckle.

Molly's gaze was drawn back to their dinner guest.

Not notice! There was no way women hadn't been noticing this man from the moment he began shaving, a task that the shadow on his firm angular jaw suggested he had not performed since at least that morning.

Casting a covert look at the newcomer through her lashes, she noted the rest of his skin was the shade of vibrant gold and blemish-free if you discounted a fine white scar that began just beneath one razor-sharp cheekbone and terminated at the corner of his wide, mobile and almost indecently sensual mouth.

Actually there was no almost about it—his mouth was indecent. The maverick thoughts that popped into her head when she looked at it certainly were!

His strongly delineated brows were the same raven shade as his hair, which looked like black satin and touched the collar of the open-necked shirt he wore. Under the layer of red dust the shirt might be the same colour as his eyes, though she doubted it—that unique shade of blue was not one that would be easy to duplicate.

Fortunately nobody seemed to notice her compulsion to look

at him as her eyes roamed across the angles and strong planes of his face. She was staring, but how could she not? Beauty was a term that people flung around casually but here was someone who actually merited the description, although not in a Hollywood type of way. The newcomer had looks that affected the onlooker on a much earthier and more primal level.

Or maybe it's just me, she thought.

It was a worrying thought, but she doubted her reaction was unique. She doubted any woman would not be inclined to stare open-mouthed when they saw the six feet four inches of lean muscle and hard sinew that was Tair Al Sharif. He really was the most extraordinary-looking man Molly had ever seen.

But the prim voice in her head reminded her that looks were not everything.

It was something her father, thinking he was being kind, had told her frequently as she grew up beside two stepsisters who were as beautiful as they were lovely-natured. Sometimes, Molly reflected, it would have been easier if Rosie and Sue had been mean and nasty. At least then she could have been jealous without feeling guilty. And there was something much more romantic about being oppressed and exploited by mean stepsisters than spoilt and indulged and told you were lovely inside.

Only last month Rosie had offered her a makeover when she had wailed in frustration that she'd prefer to be lovely on the outside and happily exchange ten points of her impressive IQ for another inch on her flat chest.

She snapped out of her reverie and drew herself back to the present to respond to Tariq. 'I completely understand why Khalid said what he did. Please tell him not to worry. However, I don't think the prince…' She stopped, realising this did not narrow the field much in the circles she was currently moving in, where princes were pretty thick on the

ground! She gave a rueful grin as she added, 'Your cousin—
I don't think he likes me much.'

The grin died as she recalled sensing, *feeling*, his extraordinary and unbelievably eloquent eyes upon her.

'Tair?' Tariq said, shaking his head. 'You must be mistaken.
He does not know you. Why should he dislike you?'

Good question, but Molly knew there had been no ambiguity
about the message she had seen in those glittering azure depths.

Having never in her life inspired any strong feelings in
gorgeous-looking men—obviously they remained oblivious
to the fact she was lovely inside—to have someone looking
at her with that level of hostility and contempt had been quite
disturbing.

His face floated into her mind gain; she tried to expel the
image but it lingered. It was a face with a 'once seen never
forgotten' quality. Even if you wanted to forget the golden skin
stretched over hard angles and intriguing hollows, the sensual
mouth and searing blue stare.

'You must have been mistaken, Molly.'

'I expect so,' she said, already wishing she had not introduced
the subject. But no matter what Tariq said she knew she was not
mistaken—Tair Al Sharif could not stand the sight of her.

Not that she was going to lose any sleep over his opinion
of her. As first impressions went she hadn't taken to him either.

'If it will make you feel better I will explain our relationship to him straight away.'

'There's really no need.' She wondered if the flicker she
saw in her brother's eyes was relief. The possibility
shouldn't have hurt, but it did. 'And I'd actually prefer if
you didn't.'

On a practical level she knew the searing dislike she had read
in the Arab prince's face was not going to alter just because he
knew she was Tariq and Khalid's English half-sister.

No, it had been loathing at first sight.

Besides, there were some people you didn't want to like you, and he was one of them, she decided. She mentally ticked off the qualities that made him undesirable—off-the-scale arrogance, no sense of humour, and he was in love with himself. The last seemed a reasonable assumption to Molly, who reasoned a person who looked at that face in the mirror every day would have to be just a little fond of himself.

'It is up to you, Molly, but what I came to say to you is that it is not a relationship that we are ashamed to acknowledge, quite the contrary…though,' Tariq conceded with a grimace, 'obviously it would be difficult to go public because…'

'This isn't easy for your father.'

Tariq looked grateful for her understanding of the situation. 'It was hard for him when our mother left… He is a proud man and the scandal of a divorce in our society, the gossip and stories, left its mark.'

It had been hard for Tariq too, but this was something Molly had not appreciated until very recently.

'Your father has been very kind to me and I wouldn't do anything to embarrass him. I'm not about to go public. I promise you I won't breathe a word to a soul. If anyone asks I'm Bea's friend.'

It was not a hard promise to make, as the level of hospitality she had received from the king had touched her deeply. However, she realised it could not be easy for him to have his ex-wife's child as a guest.

Molly knew enough about Zarhat culture to recognise that when Tariq had touched on the subject of the royal divorce he had, if anything, been downplaying the situation, yet the king had welcomed her into his home when many in his position might not have even wanted reminding of her existence.

Her solemnity as she made her vow of silence brought an

affectionate smile to Tariq's face 'I appreciate that, Molly. But you do know that Khalid and I would both have been proud to have introduced you as our sister tonight.'

Warm moisture filled Molly's amber eyes as emotion clogged her throat. 'Really…?'

'You can doubt this?' he asked, before a spasm of self-condemnation twisted his dark features. 'Of course you can. Why would you not after I have ignored you for the past twenty-four years? If you had told me to go to hell it would have been what I deserved.'

A grin spread across Molly's face as she flicked away a strand of waist-length hair that had drifted across her face. It was still slightly damp from the shower. 'The way I recall it I pretty much did just that.'

The reminder of that meeting brought a rueful grin to his face.

'If it wasn't for Beatrice coming to see me I wouldn't be here now,' she said frankly.

It was true. When the half-brother who had ignored her since birth had suggested they should get to know one another, her response had been to angrily reject his overtures. What did she need with a brother who she knew had caused their mother so much heartache by refusing any contact with her after her second marriage to Molly's father?

They were strangers and Molly had been happy for it to stay that way; she'd wanted nothing to do with him.

Why would she?

She owed Tariq nothing. He hadn't just ignored the fact she existed, he had pressured Khalid, whom she had seen and adored as a small child before their mother's premature death, to reject her too.

It had been a visit in person from Beatrice pleading her husband's case that had persuaded her to accept the invitation.

Molly had come prepared, almost wanting, to despise this

brother, but to her amazement after a slightly rocky start she had found herself liking Tariq.

'And you are glad you did come?'

Molly uncurled her legs from underneath her as she lifted her chin and scanned the lean dark face of the brother she still barely knew. 'Very glad,' she admitted huskily.

Tariq smiled and got to his feet. 'And you will think about what I have said?'

'I will,' she promised, walking with him to the door.

'Tariq!'

Standing framed in the doorway, he turned back.

'I do understand, you know…why you wouldn't come and visit Mum when she was alive.'

She hadn't always. As a small child the only thing she had understood was the desperate hurt in her mother's eyes when the eldest son she had been forced to leave behind when she'd divorced the King of Zarhat had not accompanied his brother for the arranged visit.

It had not crossed her mind at the time that Tariq had been hurting too and perhaps feeling betrayed that the mother he had loved had chosen her freedom over her sons.

'Dad told me, when he knew I was coming here, how she never stopped feeling guilty about leaving you and Khalid, but she knew you would be safe and loved. She always knew that your place was here.'

'And hers was not.'

There was no trace of criticism in Tariq's manner but Molly felt impelled to defend the choice their mother had made.

'She must have been very desperate.'

Molly could only imagine the sort of unhappiness that would make a woman make that choice. She knew nothing about the strength of maternal bonds, but something deep inside her told her that to leave a child would be like ripping away part of yourself and you'd walk around with that awful emptiness the rest of your life.

Without being judgemental, Molly really couldn't imagine a situation where she would make the same decision.

'But she knew you and Khalid would be well cared for and I think me being here would have made her very happy.'

Without a word Molly stepped into arms that opened for her and the years of rejection and anger melted away.

'God, look at me, I'm crying,' she said as she emerged from a crushing brotherly hug. She wiped the moisture from her face with one hand and pushed back her hair with the other.

'Go on,' she sniffed. 'Or Beatrice will be sending out the search party.'

CHAPTER TWO

FROM where he was standing, Tair witnessed the embrace and heard Molly's parting warning. He could feel the anger burning inside him like a solid physical presence.

He stayed where he stood concealed in the shadows until the echoes of Tariq's footsteps on the marble floor died away. Then he began to walk towards the door that had just closed, his long stride filled with purpose.

A muscle clenched in his firm jaw as he imagined her in the room feeling pleased with herself because nobody suspected her game. Her mask was good, he conceded, but he had seen through her disguise.

There was no effort involved in recreating in his head the image of her standing in the doorway.

He had barely recognised the mouse minus the glasses and with her hair hanging loose to her narrow waist like a silken screen. The light streaming from the bedroom had acted like a spotlight shining through the fine fabric of her demure nightclothes, revealing every dip and curve of a slender but undeniably female form. Female enough to cause a lustful surge of his own undiscriminating hormones.

Who would have guessed, other than Tariq, that under the baggy top there was that body?

He stopped a few feet from the door and forced himself to think past both the memory of those small plump breasts and his anger—the two seemed inextricably linked in his head— and took a deep breath, forcing the fury boiling in his veins to a gentle simmer.

To confront her would give him pleasure of a sort, but what would it achieve? Other than to watch her struggle as she tried to explain away what he had seen. She would have her work cut out, Tair thought. He was not a man to jump to conclusions, but in this instance he felt he was fully justified to assume the worst.

However, what he had witnessed showed how deeply she had her unvarnished claws into Tariq, and threats from him were not going to make her back off. Him barging in might even have the opposite effect and actually make the situation worse. Right now the situation was retrievable, but if the affair became public knowledge…?

He needed to think. He needed to think about this like any other problem. He needed to analyse the problem, decide what he wanted to happen and then choose how he was going to make it happen.

Tair inhaled deeply, then released the breath slowly. With one last look at the door he turned and strode away in the opposite direction to the one his cousin had taken.

Tariq, who had been walking across the courtyard, stopped when he saw his cousin. 'Tair!'

Tair stepped towards him thinking, You idiot, as he smiled. Tariq looked exhausted. Perhaps guilt made him lie awake at night?

He too had lain awake the previous night, but he was not feeling any effects from the lack of sleep; he was actually feeling quite pleased with himself.

Some might consider his plan reckless, but Tair preferred to think of it as inspired.

'I'm glad I bumped into you.'

The relief he saw on the other man's face struck Tair as darkly ironic.

'Actually—' Tariq, his brow furrowed, glanced down at the watch on his wrist '—you could do me a favour. I don't suppose you would take a message to Molly for me?'

Tair inclined his head to indicate his willingness to help out and thought that this was working out much better than he'd anticipated.

It wasn't very often the victim of a scam actively helped facilitate the scheme. Not that he had a lot of personal experience with scams, and this was one being perpetuated with the most altruistic of motives. He didn't expect that Tariq would immediately be able to make the differentiation, though obviously when he had come to his senses he would appreciate his good fortune.

'You'll find her in the glasshouses,' he explained, glancing down at his watch in a manner that seemed uncharacteristically distracted to Tair. 'She's interested in that sort of thing. Well, she would be, wouldn't she?'

'She would?' Tair, who was mentally bringing forward his plan by an hour, pretended an interest he did not feel.

'Well, yes, she's head of the science department but her first degree was in botany. When I told her about the glasshouses built by great-grandfather and his collection she was fascinated. I was looking for Khalid to do the honours for me, but I can't track him down.'

'She is a teacher?' he said, unable to hide his doubt. Surely in order to command the respect of pupils a teacher needed to project an air of authority?

Tariq looked amused. 'Have you spoken to her at all? She

teaches at a girls' school.' He named a prestigious establish-
ment that even Tair had heard of and added, 'Molly is really
very bright,' He said this with an obvious pride that set Tair's
teeth on edge.

'I know she seems quiet, but once you start talking to
her…she's actually got a great sense of humour and—'

'She seems to have a most articulate advocate in you,' Tair
cut in before his cousin waxed even more lyrical and was
unable to keep a guard on his tongue. 'I will,' he promised,
'certainly make the effort to know her better.' He knew all he
needed to know about Miss Mouse.

'So we have you for a few more days?'

'My travel plans are not certain yet,' Tair lied, thinking of
his refuelled plane and freshly charted flightplan.

'Tell Molly I'm sorry, but I'll have to take a rain check. Bea
had a bad night. They think it's a good idea if she checks into
the hospital.' He glanced down at his watch again. 'I've been
banished while she packs a bag. She says I'm driving her mad
fussing.' Despite his joking tone the lines of strain around his
mouth made it clear that Tariq was worried.

'You should have said something!' Tair exclaimed. 'Is
she—?'

'It's just a precaution,' Tariq cut in quickly. 'Her blood
pressure is up a little and, well, the fact is she's been doing
too much. It's my fault—I shouldn't have left her alone.'

Tair thought it was a little late for the other man to realise
this, but given his obvious agitation it seemed unnecessarily
cruel to labour the point so he contented himself with an
abrupt, 'Your place is with your wife.'

'So you'll explain the situation to Molly?'

Could he not forget the woman even now? 'I will make sure
she understands.'

Tariq laid a hand on his arm. 'Thanks, Tair, and try not to scare her. Poor Molly has the impression you can't stand the sight of her.'

The girl was highly perceptive, Tair thought, while lifting his brows in an attitude of amazement.

'I know, crazy,' Tariq remarked with an indulgent smile that made Tair's teeth grate, 'but I think you make her nervous… I know you can be charming, Tair, and I'd be grateful if you'd make the effort for me. This is her first visit here and I want her to come back.'

Not if I have anything to say about it. 'For you, yes, cousin, I will make the effort.'

'Thanks for this, Tair.'

'It is my pleasure.' And if not his pleasure, it was certainly his duty to remove temptation from Tariq's way.

The perfectly preserved glasshouses built in the Victorian era covered acres of ground and they contained not only historical and rare fruit and vegetable varieties, but a unique and priceless collection of orchids.

Tair was familiar with the glasshouses as when he was a boy visiting his cousins they had played there. It took him a short time to locate Molly, though he almost walked past her, only catching sight of the shiny top of her head at the last minute.

He backtracked and saw she was sitting on the floor with her knees drawn up, her attention divided between the sketchbook balanced on her knee and an orchid in full fragrant bloom. Its heady scent filled the air around them.

She was so intent on her task that she didn't hear his approach and as she continued to remain unaware of his presence Tair had the opportunity to study her unobserved.

Her body was hidden once more behind another unattractive outfit—an oversized shirt and shapeless skirt that reached mid-calf. But his attention remained on her face. Like last night, she was not wearing the librarian glasses, but unlike last night he was close enough to appreciate the delicacy of her bone structure and the smooth creaminess of her skin. Still oblivious to his presence, she turned her head as she laid down the pencil in her hand to pick up another from the tin that lay open beside her and he was able to see that her face was a perfect oval.

Her delicate winged brows drew together in a frown of concentration as she turned her attention back to the drawing, her slim fingers flying over the paper.

When she finished the frown deepened into a grimace of dissatisfaction as she compared what was on the paper to the waxy petalled bloom she was studying.

'Hopeless!' she muttered in apparent disgust at her inability to do her subject justice.

'A lack of talent can be frustrating.'

She started as though shot and turned her head jerkily, causing several strands of hair to break loose from the knot tied at the base of her slender neck. Their eyes connected and Tair was struck by two thoughts simultaneously. Her eyes were pure gold and she was looking at him as though he were, if not the devil himself, then certainly a very close relation. She appeared not to notice as the pencil slipped from her nerveless fingers and slid into the decorative grating of an air vent.

He raised one brow and she astonished him by blushing to the roots of her hair. Hair that turned out not to be boring mousy brown, but a subtle combination of shades ranging from soft gold to warm conker.

The knot on the nape of her neck appeared to be secured by a single barrette; presumably if it was removed her hair would spill like silk down her back.

Had Tariq done this?

He pushed the thought away, baring his teeth in a smile. Tariq wouldn't be doing that or anything else that involved Miss Mouse any more.

Even before she turned Molly had known who was standing there. Tair Al Sharif's voice had to be just about the most distinctive on the planet! He could have made the ingredients on a cereal packet sound like an indecent proposition. The velvet smoothness had an almost tactile quality that sent tiny secret shivers up and down her spine.

Even when he stopped speaking she could hear it in her head.

Molly kept her head down and got to her feet slowly to allow the heat in her cheeks time to dissipate.

Even when she was standing straight he remained a full foot, probably more, taller than her. Molly would have liked to believe it was simply the extra inches alone that made her feel at such a disadvantage. But even without looking directly at him she could feel the effect of the leashed power and blatantly sexual aura he radiated lying like a stone fist in her chest. It made her conscious of each breath she took.

He was dressed smart-casual, or in his case sexy-casual, in jeans, secured across his lean snaky hips with a leather belt, and a blue open-necked shirt.

Molly had never thought before that the words denim and disturbing could be in the same sentence as she glanced at the way the material clung to his long muscular thighs.

Last night Molly had tossed and turned in bed unable to get this man's voice or face from her mind although she had tried to blame her inability to sleep on the second cup of coffee she'd had at dinner.

At about two a.m. she had decided that she had imagined the hypnotic quality of his searing blue eyes and the inexplicable hostility she saw in them when they were turned in her direction.

Now a caffeine-free zone, she had to admit she had been fooling herself.

Even after having adjusted her stare to a point over his shoulder she could feel his eyes on her. The sort of eyes that layers of skin and bone seemed a poor defence against—it felt as if he could see inside her skull.

When she was this close to him she felt as though every protective layer she had built up over the years had been peeled away. Chastising herself crossly at the whimsical illusion, she kept staring into the safety zone over his shoulder, deciding it was preferable to have him assume she was cross-eyed than maintain direct eye contact and do something stupid like trip over her own feet, drool or forget her name.

This is stupid—you look ridiculous, Molly thought. Look at the man—you can't talk to the wall! Surely nothing should scare a person who had stood in at the last minute for an absent colleague and delivered a sex-education lecture to a hall of sixteen-year-old girls?

It had turned out the girls knew a lot more than she did!

'You startled me,' she said, brushing the dust off the seat of her skirt before tucking a stray strand of hair behind her ear. 'I didn't hear you.' And if I had I would have run in the opposite direction.

It was still an option, she thought, staring at his shiny boots.

'Sorry,' he said, not looking it, but not actually sounding as openly antagonistic as he had the previous evening.

It was possible she'd been wrong about the hostility, not that he had the sort of face that was easy to read if he didn't want you to. And right now it would seem he didn't want her to.

Her gaze flickered across the hard contours and angles of his lean face and a sigh snagged in her throat. He might not be easy to read, but he was damned easy to look at! A lot more than easy!

Her glance dropped to his feet shod in leather boots and then, as though drawn by an invisible magnet, worked its way upwards, lingering over some areas more than others, until she reached his face. Everything about him was worth looking at.

She applied the tip of her tongue to the moisture that broke out along her upper lip and struggled to disguise the fact that her feet were nailed to the ground with lust.

No man had ever elicited this type of raw response from Molly in her life and she found it both utterly mortifying and deeply scary.

As he reached across to take the sketch-book from her she opened her mouth to protest but nothing came out. With fingers clenched almost as tight as her teeth, she injected amusement into her voice as she held out her hand.

'I doubt my scribbling will interest you, Mr al… Prince…'

His eyes lifted, meeting hers momentarily. He ignored the hand. 'Or my opinion interest you?'

'I'm holding my breath.' Actually the entire breathing thing was currently something of a chore. She was twenty-four and had never been in a situation where sexual awareness caused her brain to malfunction before.

The acid sweetness of her retort caused his eyes to narrow before they dropped. Biting her lip, Molly watched in dismay as Tair Al Sharif, his dark head tilted a little to one side, continued to study the sketch.

So far he hadn't been overly impressed by anything about her, so why, she asked herself dourly, should now be any different?

She stopped and blinked… Will you just listen to yourself, Molly? Have you any idea how pathetic and needy you sound?

She took a deep breath, lifted her chin and advised herself

sternly to grow up. For goodness' sake, he was not an art critic. Why should she give a damn what he thought?

She didn't!

So why was she standing here shuffling her feet like a kid called to the headmaster's study?

This was ridiculous. She was acting like some needy loser who wanted everyone to love her… Someone might be nice, but that someone was not going to bear any resemblance to Tair Al Sharif.

The internal dialogue came to an abrupt end as he lifted his raven head.

He was surprised that she actually did have the talent he accused her of lacking, a fact that was obvious even to his un-educated eye. The drawing leapt off the paper. It was detailed and delicate and if it did not meet with her approval the artist was an extremely harsh critic of her own skills.

He removed his eyes from the sketch-book and turned his attention to her, his dark gaze drifting over the outfit that was not what most women would have selected for a meeting with a lover, but clearly Tariq was able to see past the dowdy disguise. The thought of his smitten cousin brought a dark scowl of disapproval to his face and it was still in place when their eyes connected.

Molly went to push up the glasses on her nose only to discover they weren't there. She experienced a moment of total panic, the sort she felt in nightmares.

She didn't need his approval, she told herself sternly, and she didn't need a safety blanket either. The glasses had been useful once, but she was no longer a precociously bright but gauche kid plunged into the university environment among people who were older.

Tair had seen the gesture. 'You have mislaid your specta-cles… Can you not see without them?' It amused him that the teacher was looking at him as though she were a pupil expecting a reprimand from a headmaster.

She gave a shrug. 'They'll turn up.'

'The picture is very good.' He handed back the sketchbook, which she took and slowly closed.

A gratified smile lifted the corners of her sensual lips, and her eyes looked like polished amber as they shone with pleasure. The permanent groove above his hawklike nose deepened. Her reaction struck him as a wildly over-the-top response to what had been a grudging observation.

As if the same thought had suddenly occurred to her, the smile vanished and she lowered her eyes. 'Thank you.'

CHAPTER THREE

'I CANNOT be the first person to tell you that you have...talent.'

The harsh emphasis Tair placed on the last word confused Molly. 'It's a hobby...it's just for my own amusement.'

And did it amuse her to steal another woman's husband? The muscles of his brown throat worked as he regarded her with distaste.

His rigid disapproving stance made her shift uncomfortably, and she dropped her gaze. Seeing her glasses lying on the floor, she bent to pick them up with a grunt of relief. Unfortunately Tair did too, his brown fingertips brushing the skin of her wrist as he reached them just before her.

The brief contact sent a surge of tingling sensation through her body. She stepped back, almost stumbled, then, breathing hard, she straightened up.

Tair watched as she nursed one hand against her chest, his eyes drawn to the visibly throbbing blue-veined pulse spot at the base of her throat.

The air was dense with a sexual tension you could have reached out and grabbed with both hands. It hung in the hot, humid air like a crackling field of electricity.

Tair viewed this unexpected development with as much objectivity as he was able—which wasn't very much when he was seeing life through a hot hormonal haze.

It hadn't been slow burn, it had just exploded out of nowhere and it still held him in its grip.

Tair's jaw clenched as he struggled to reassert control; he was not a man who let his appetites rule him. Of course he had experienced his share of lustful moments but he'd never been drawn to anyone in such an elemental way before.

This personal insight into what this woman could do to a man ought to have made him feel sympathy for his cousin, but it was not empathy he felt when he thought of Tariq following up on the sort of impulse he had just resisted.

Resisted, even though he was free to follow his urges, unlike his cousin.

His hooded gaze slid to her mouth.

'It's just for my own amusement,' she repeated hoarsely.

His own amusement was very much in Tair's thoughts as his eyes stayed on the soft full outline of her lips. If he followed up on his impulses it would be because he chose to and not because he couldn't help himself.

He had control.

So why had he been staring at her mouth for the last two minutes as if it were an oasis and he were a man who needed water?

Hands clenched at his sides, he removed his eyes from her lips. If he did kiss her it would be at a time and place of his choosing.

Pushing back strands of loose hair from her brow, Molly extended her hand towards him. 'Thank you...'

As he looked at her fingertips Tair thought about them trailing over his damp bare skin. A spasm of irritation drew his lean features into a frown. His problem was that there had been too much work in his life recently and not enough sex.

His problem, he acknowledged, was her mouth.

* * *

To Molly's utter dismay, instead of handing her the spectacles Tair held them up to his own eyes.

She watched his dark brows lift towards his hairline and thought how it was typical that the only person who had ever seen past her harmless charade had to be him.

'Clear glass…?'

He struggled to hide his extreme distaste at his discovery. Presumably the clothes and unmade face were all part of the same illusion. The one that made other women dismiss her as no threat, but every man she came into contact with knew different.

He knew different.

Molly, feeling an irrational level of guilt as though she had been caught out in some shameful crime, shook her head mutely.

She was not about to explain that when arriving at university via an educational hothouse scheme for gifted children, aged sixteen and looking fourteen, she had come up with the inspired idea of looking older by adopting a pair of heavy spectacles. She realised now that they hadn't made her look older but over the years they had become a safety blanket.

'A fashion accessory.'

'I think you should change your fashion guru.'

The suggestion drew a forced laugh from Molly. 'Fashion isn't really my thing.'

'But wearing clothes two sizes too big is?'

He didn't come right out and say that she looked like a dowdy bag lady, but that was clearly the message in his comment. The voltage of Molly's smile went up and her muscles ached from the fixed and slightly inane grin her facial muscles had frozen into.

She was comfortable in her own skin, and if this man with his perfect face and better than perfect body couldn't see past superficial things like make-up and clothes that was his problem. She only had a problem if she started caring what men she met casually thought about her.

It could be she had a problem.

She looked at his fingers holding her glasses. They were rather incredible; long, tapering and the lightest contact with them had sent her nervous system into meltdown. She was sure there was a perfectly logical explanation for what happened—a build-up of static electricity and a freakish set of circumstances that couldn't be repeated if she tried.

But Molly wasn't about to put her theory to the test. As far as Prince Tair was concerned she had a strict no-touch policy—her body was still shaken by intermittent aftershocks from his light touch. Anything more intimate and she might well end up hospitalised.

Just as well him getting more intimate with her was about as likely as snow in the desert.

With the fixed smile still painted in place, she reached out to carefully take her glasses from his fingers.

He gave a sardonic smile that Molly didn't choose to respond to, her cheeks pink as she slid the spectacles onto her nose while expelling a shaky sigh of relief. Of course he knew he was gorgeous. Of course he knew women fainted away when he deigned to throw them a smile, but, God, she didn't want to be one of them.

It was all so shallow and silly. It seemed a good moment to remind herself that she was neither.

'I'm meeting Tariq,' she explained, hoping he would take the hint and go away. There were only so many times a girl could make a fool of herself. 'He should be here any minute now.'

'I know.'

'You do?' Then why hadn't he just said so straight off instead of giving her the opportunity to act like a total imbecile?

'He asked me to deliver a message.'

She gave an encouraging nod. Dragging a sentence out of this man was like dragging blood from the proverbial stone.

'He is not coming.'

Molly's face fell. 'Right, well…thank you.' She urged him to go—her system couldn't take all this undiluted testosterone.

'Beatrice is not well.'

Molly's mask fell away. 'Beatrice…' She pressed one hand to her mouth and, all hint of self-preservation gone, she caught his arm with the other. 'What happened?' she asked, her mind turning over the events of two days earlier when she had come across Beatrice sitting with her head between her knees recovering from a slight dizzy spell.

Molly's first inclination had been to get help, but Bea had begged her not to, saying that Tariq was already wildly over-protective and he would worry himself silly over a moment of light-headedness.

She shouldn't have let Bea dissuade her, she thought. She should have told Tariq.

Tair felt the fingers curled over his forearm tighten.

'Apparently she had a…troubled night.'

'Troubled? What do you mean troubled?'

Anyone who hadn't seen Tariq come out of her room the previous night might have believed that wide-eyed concern. The mouse was clearly a very good actress, although earlier she had not been good enough to hide her response to his touch. The shocked expression in her widely dilated eyes had been a total give-away.

'The doctor came this morning.'

'Doctor…oh, God!'

Tair watched the rest of the colour leave her face. Her fainting on him hadn't been any part of his plan.

'And he advised she be transferred to hospital.' Presumably her reaction had more to do with guilt than genuine concern, or if it was it was a very selective form of that sentiment.

'Is she…is the baby…? She hasn't gone into labour yet?' She quickly reminded herself that lots of babies were born perfectly healthily at thirty-five weeks.

'As far as I know it is just a precaution…?' He deliberately injected a questioning note into his voice.

Molly let go of his arm and lifted a hand to her head. Closing her eyes, she leaned back against a tier of elaborately carved cast-iron shelves spilling with lush greenery. 'This is my fault.'

Tair saw no reason to let her off the hook. If she was beginning to realise that her selfish actions had consequences it was long overdue, he thought grimly.

'What makes you say that?'

She inhaled deeply and opened her eyes. 'A few days ago Bea sort of fainted—well, she said not, but I think she did. She asked me not to say anything to Tariq… I knew I should have told him…' She shook her head and gave a self-recriminatory grimace as she slapped the heel of her hand hard against her forehead. 'If she's ill, if anything happens to the baby, it's my fault.'

She was either a brilliant actress—and no one was that brilliant—or this woman had a seriously skewed take on morality. How could she care about the wife and cheat with the husband?

'Do you know what's wrong? Is there something you're hiding? Is Bea in danger?'

He shrugged. 'I'm not hiding anything. Tariq wasn't that forthcoming.'

'He must be frantic!' If anything happened to Bea or the baby she knew he would be utterly devastated. Her half-brother's obvious adoration of his wife had been one of the first things that had made her warm towards him.

'I'm going out to the hospital so I could take you if you like? I'm sure you will be a great comfort to Tariq.'

Molly, deaf to the ironic inflection in his steely addition, turned to him with a beam of gratitude.

'Really?'

'I'm sure Beatrice would like to have such an old friend around.'

She smiled and reached out impulsively to touch his arm again as she said, 'It really is kind of you.' Then Molly saw he was looking at her hand and with a self-conscious grimace she let it fall away.

'Not kind.'

The strange way he said it made her throw him a frowning look of enquiry, but his expression told her nothing.

'Come.'

Molly responded to the command, falling into step beside him as he went through a door that linked the glasshouses with the main building. 'I was thinking, perhaps I should ring the hospital? They must have left in a hurry. Maybe,' she mused, quickening her pace to keep up with Tair's longer stride, 'there is something Bea would like me to bring for her…'

Molly knew if the positions were reversed she would like to have a few personal things around her to make her hospital room seem more homely.

'There is no shortage of people to bring the princess what she needs.'

Molly gave a rueful grimace and felt foolish. 'Of course there is. I just can't get used to that.'

'To what?'

'The fact that there are people to tie her shoelaces if she wants.' And Beatrice seemed so normal.

'I forget that you knew Beatrice before she was married. Have you been friends long?'

Molly, never comfortable with the lie, shrugged and mumbled, 'It feels like for ever.' Which was true; her rapport with Beatrice had been instant. She doubted she could have felt closer if Bea had been one of her own sisters.

When they reached the courtyard a four-wheel drive was waiting there for them. Tair spoke to the man behind the wheel, who got out and, with a courteous nod in her direction, retreated.

'I prefer to drive myself.'

Molly dragged her eyes from the vehicle to the man she was going to share it with and felt her stomach muscles tighten nervously. Suddenly this didn't seem like such a brilliant idea.

'Should I change?' she asked, lifting a hand to her head. 'I should probably tidy up and get something to cover my hair. Look, you don't have to wait for me—you go. I'll make my own way to the hospital.'

'You look fine as you are.'

Tair slid into the driving seat but still Molly hung back. She recognised the reason for her reluctance and knew it was ridiculous, but the thought of being in an enclosed confine with this man and his sexual magnetism scared her witless.

Though wasn't magnetism meant to work both ways? If so this must be something else because he wasn't drawn in her direction, reluctantly or any other way!

He glanced across at her, with one dark brow elevated, looking more like a dark fallen angel than ever. 'Are you coming?'

'I was just…' She stopped, her eyes sliding from his as she realised she could hardly tell him his aggressive masculinity made her feel raw and uncomfortably vulnerable.

A spasm of irritation crossed his dark features as she continued to hesitate. 'Do you want this lift or not?'

Molly told herself to calm down. This was just a lift; she wasn't signing away her life. All she had to do for Tariq and Bea was to survive for twenty minutes in this man's company.

'Well, if it's no bother.'

CHAPTER FOUR

MOLLY had assumed that Tair was taking a short cut to the airport when he turned off onto a dirt track, but after they had been travelling for forty minutes it occurred to her that short cuts were meant to be...well...shorter.

Were they lost?

They hit another bump in the road and Molly let out an involuntary little cry as she was jolted.

He flicked her a brief sideways glance. 'Are you all right?'

'Fine.'

Tair turned his attention back to the road and she slid a covert look at his patrician profile. He didn't look like someone who didn't have a clue where he was. He looked like someone who always knew exactly where he was going. On the other hand, she supposed, men were notoriously reluctant to admit when they were lost.

Her lips curved into a secret smile as she looked at him and thought how he was definitely *all* man. The gusty sigh that lifted her chest caused his eyes to find her face once more.

'Are you sure you're all right?'

'I bit my tongue, that's all.'

Feeling the guilty heat rise to her cheeks, she fixed her gaze on her hands clasped primly in her lap. Adjusting her regard onto the arid scenery they were driving through, she thought how there wasn't a single landmark in the miles and miles of featureless desert. It had to be very easy to miss a turning out here. It wasn't as if there were signposts or, for that matter, anything else.

She averted her gaze from the bleak landscape with a shudder, unable to see the beauty in this empty land that Beatrice spoke of. Presumably her mother had seen no appeal in it either.

'I suppose satellite navigation must be essential out here,' she remarked casually. The vehicle they were in was equipped with it, but Tair had not switched it on.

His broad shoulders lifted in a shrug. 'Useful, I suppose, if you are not accustomed to negotiating the desert terrain.'

'Which you are?'

'Which I am,' he agreed. 'It is in my blood.'

Molly could have listed the constituents of blood and to her knowledge the items would not include a sense of direction. She kept a discreet silence on the subject but possibly her scepticism showed because he volunteered further information to back up his claim.

'My mother came from a Bedouin tribe, and my grandfather is the sheikh of his tribe.'

Her eyes widened. As she glanced at him it was impossible not to see him as a romantic figure in flowing desert robes. 'People still live that way?'

'The tribal way of life is dying out,' he admitted.

It was hard to tell from his expression if he considered this a bad thing or not.

'But there are some like my grandfather who keep tradition alive.'

'Your grandfather is alive?'

He flashed her a grin and for a brief moment looked less

austere and stern. 'My grandfather is very much alive, but Mother died when I was a child.'

'Mine too.' Which was about the only thing they could possibly have in common.

'You have no family?'

Her eyes dropped as she shook her head. 'Dad is alive and I have two stepsisters, and two half-brothers.'

His brows lifted. 'A large family.'

Families were a place Molly did not want to go! She was beginning to wish she had stuck to a safer subject like the weather.

'Big queues for the bathroom,' she said, trying to close down the subject, though she couldn't help but wonder what his reaction would be if she said, Actually I'm Tariq and Khalid's half-sister—my mother divorced the king.

His blue eyes looked over at her face. 'But you could not have been lonely growing up.'

Did that mean he had been? Did lonely little boys turn into men as self-reliant as this one? Despite the extreme unlikelihood of this, an image of a dark-haired little boy with lonely blue eyes flashed into her head. The sort of little boy you'd want to pull into your arms.

Only, little boys you wanted to hug grew up into men around whom it would be wise to keep such impulses under control!

Besides, she thought, her glance drifting towards his powerful shoulders, relaxed despite the rough terrain he was negotiating, it was obvious that there wouldn't be many people who could pull him any place he didn't want to go these days!

He was far more likely to be the one doing the pulling and very few women she could think of would do any resisting!

Her lashes brushed her cheeks as, eyes half closed, she wondered what it would feel like to have those arms close around her. Her eyes darted, as though drawn by an invisible force, to his mouth, her pupil dilating dramatically as she stared at the sculpted outline. It was a fascinating combination of passion and control. A fractured gasp locked in her throat and she pressed a hand against the pounding pulse at the base of her neck.

How would it feel to be claimed by that mouth? She ran a finger across the upper curve of her lips and thought it would surely be pretty mind-blindingly sensational.

God, what was she doing?

She was weaving a sexual fantasy about someone she didn't even like doing something he was never going to do. Men like Tair Al Sharif did not kiss women like her.

But if he did?

The question popped unbidden into her head and once it was there it wouldn't go away, even when she tore her eyes from his mouth.

They hit another pothole and Molly, teeth gritted and eyes trained on the dusty track ahead, barely noticed—even though her seat belt cut painfully into her shoulder. She picked up the thread of their conversation.

'I wasn't lonely.'

Molly winced to hear the note of defiance in her voice. Tair had struck a sensitive nerve she hadn't known she had because she hadn't been lonely. Not as such.

How could a person be lonely with a great dad and stepsisters who never excluded her? Sue and Rosie had always gone out of their way to involve their studious, less popular little sister. The fact that she had always been conscious of a sense of being different was down to something in herself, Molly suspected.

'And I really would be a lot happier if you kept your eyes on the road—if you can call it that.' Now that she said it Molly realised that she wasn't sure there was even a track anymore. It had deteriorated over the past couple of miles to the point where it was hard to tell where it ended and the desert began.

'If I was a more suspicious man I might think you were trying to change the subject.'

The man was far too perceptive. 'No, I simply don't want to arrive at the hospital in need of medical attention,' she retorted tartly while thinking psychiatric analysis might not be such a bad idea.

She lasted thirty seconds before she responded to the over-powering compulsion to look at him. She was studying the strong, aggressively male curve of his jaw from beneath the concealing sweep of her lashes when he turned his head. Caught staring like a child in a sweet shop, Molly fought the impulse not to look away guiltily.

He smiled the sort of smile that suggested it wasn't anything new for him to have women stare in lustful longing at him, which it no doubt wasn't, but that in her eyes did not excuse the arrogance. In fact it made it worse!

She cringed inwardly imagining him thinking she was a pushover—another one unable to resist his alpha-male mag-netism.

Insufferable egotist!

'I was just wondering…' if you're as good at kissing as you look? '…if your male ego…' she choked as her colour height-ened '…would take a bashing if I asked you if we're lost?'

He grinned again and Molly thought he really should do that more often.

'My ego is pretty robust, but thank you for caring.'

She'd never seriously thought any different—he hardly looked as if he had a self-esteem issue. 'I don't,' she muttered under her breath.

She was relieved when Tair showed no sign of hearing her childish retort. She wasn't childish, or inarticulate, and she definitely wasn't sex-starved—well, only out of choice and it had never felt like a problem before—so why was it she displayed all these embarrassing characteristics around this man?

'So I'll risk it. Are we?'

He probably wouldn't look on getting lost in a desert as a crisis—he'd more likely relish the challenge of being forced to rely on his ingenuity to survive in a hostile environment.

A frown of dismay twitched her brows as it occurred to Molly that the thought of being lost in the desert didn't alarm her as much as it should have. A circumstance that might have something to do with whom she'd be stranded with.

'No.' He flashed her a quick sideways look.

Was she meant to find the monosyllabic response comforting? 'Then where are we?'

'We are almost there,' he said in the manner of an adult humouring an impatient child. 'In fact,' he added a moment later, 'we are there.'

She shook her head, repeated, 'There?' and looked out of the window. 'Here! This isn't an airport.'

This wasn't anything! Apart from a couple of large corrugated metal buildings that had seen better days, there seemed very little to differentiate where they were from the previous dusty miles of empty red sand they had just driven across.

The entire place seemed totally deserted—it looked like a ghost town minus the town.

'It was twenty years ago.'

She looked at his profile and the nebulous feeling of something not being quite right crystallised into fear. 'Why have you taken me here?'

As she spoke they rounded the side of the largest building and she saw a solitary plane sitting on what she supposed would once have been a runway, but which now had several visible and large potholes.

'It's all part of my devious plan to abduct you.' One dark brow elevated.

The embarrassed heat flew to Molly's cheeks. 'Sorry!' she mumbled, feeling utterly mortified that she'd questioned him.

'It's just when you said plane I assumed...' She broke off and gave an awkward shrug. 'And it did feel as if we've been driving for miles and...'

'You suspect my motives?' he suggested, not looking offended by the possibility as he brought the big vehicle to a halt a few hundred yards from the plane.

'Of course not. I'm a bit tense. The desert makes me nervous.' You make me nervous, she thought, her glance drifting to his mouth, and you make me feel other things too.

Things that brought into question Molly's deeply held belief that she could only ever be sexually attracted to someone she liked, and respected. Someone suitable. Molly simply didn't accept the idea that you had no control over the person you fell for. It was the equivalent of saying she saw a hole in the ground and she had to step into it—she didn't have to and she was never going to!

It was all about walking around the obstacle. So far her life had been obstacle-free—depressingly so, it seemed at times, but when she saw one heading her way she was going to get out of the way!

Molly could see how the rule might be bent a little if both parties were just after casual sex, but she had more or less ruled that out a long time ago as not really being her.

As she slid a sideways look at her companion she doubted he shared her view of casual sex—he probably had a very high libido...

He turned his head and gave her a look of enquiry.

For a moment her brain refused to function, and the silence stretched uncomfortably.

'Where's the runway?' she finally blurted, hoping to give the impression she had been thinking hard about navigational problems and not his appetite for sex.

If he wondered why she was blushing, to her intense relief he didn't ask for enlightenment. 'Just there.'

Glad to be able to look at something that wasn't him, Molly followed the direction of his gaze to the same bumpy piece of ground she'd noticed before.

'You landed here?' she asked as she thought back to how he'd arrived at dinner last night. Her voice rose to an incredulous squeak as she added, 'In the dark?'

'Visibility was not good.'

A laugh was drawn from her throat—she had not appreciated until this moment what a master of understatement he was or how much he had played down the incident the previous evening.

She looked at the potholes in the optimistically named runway, holes that on closer inspection were more like craters, and gave a small shudder as she thought of him landing that small plane in the middle of a dust storm. He was either a very good pilot or very lucky.

Molly was sure that if she had been forced to endure similar circumstances she would be a gibbering wreck, but there had been nothing about him last night to suggest he had done anything out of the ordinary.

'There was very little option,' he told her wryly.

'For a man with nerves of steel maybe,' she said sarcastically. 'Hysterics would have worked a treat for me.'

'You don't strike me as the hysterical type.' He angled a narrow considering glance at her face. 'Hysterics require a loss of emotional control. A degree of spontaneity.'

Her firmly rounded jaw tightened in response to the cold disdain in his voice.

'And I think you're a teacher who likes to be in charge and call the shots.'

He said it without a trace of irony…it was staggering!

Her frown died as a gurgle of incredulous laughter escaped her.

'You find something amusing?'

She had seen a flash of wary caution in his eyes and was puzzled by it, but there was so much about this man that confused her that if she tried to work out what made him tick she could be here until the next century.

'You,' she admitted frankly.

The look of blank amazement her response elicited drew another gurgle of laughter from her and the dry suggestion from him she might like to elaborate.

She gave a shrug and thought it wasn't her problem if he didn't like what he heard. She had no doubt he wouldn't because, although he might be a bit unorthodox as Arab princes went, the bottom line was that he *was* an Arab prince and he took a certain amount of respect for granted.

'Me like control? This from someone who is probably the most domineering man on the planet!' And she'd only seen his royal persona. Goodness knew what he was like behind closed doors…closed bedroom doors…

She lowered her eyes to shut out the sight of his dark sardonic features and clicked her tongue pretending an amusement she was no longer feeling. 'As if you go with the flow?'

She lifted her eyes and was irrationally annoyed to see that he *was* looking amused. It goaded her on to add unwisely, 'I always think men like you are threatened by women who know their own minds.'

Looking at him through the mesh of her lashes, she saw he didn't appear very threatened, but neither was he looking pleased. She closed her mouth but almost immediately opened it again…the buzz, the adrenaline rush she got challenging him was exciting and addictive. Had she lost her mind?

'That's why they pick the ones who act as if everything they say is a pearl of wisdom.'

This went some way to explaining his hostility towards her—but she realised this theory only worked if she had come across as a woman who had a mind. The previous night she had barely said more than a few words and they were please and thank you.

She had actually acted pretty much like his perfect woman…minus the obligatory beauty. Now if she had looked like Bea…?

Well, she didn't, so she'd have to get used to it. 'At least I have a sense of humour.'

She wasn't aware that she had voiced this wistful observation out loud until Tair said, 'Tariq appears to find it one of your most attractive qualities.'

'Do you?' she blurted.

There was a long enough pause to allow Molly time to squirm and despairingly wonder why she kept saying cringing things like that.

When he finally responded there was no discernible expression on his dark, devastating features. 'No.'

It wasn't what he said or the way he said it—his voice was flat and devoid of emotion—it was where he was looking when he said it, her mouth, that made the pit of her stomach disintegrate and her temperature rise by several uncomfortable degrees.

After he delivered his flat, monosyllabic response he carried on staring. Trapped by the heat in his shimmering eyes, she stared back.

A pulse of hot liquid longing and then another and another thudded through her. She struggled with the reckless impulse to reach out and touch his lean face, to press her fingertip to the nerve that clenched spasmodically along the side of his chiselled jaw.

She lifted a hand, then, fingers clenched tight, she pressed it to her own throat. Growing dizzy, she struggled to draw adequate air into her lungs—they felt scorched by the heat that engulfed her.

Molly had no idea how long they stayed that way, but when he did speak she blinked like someone waking up. The question was what was she waking from—a nightmare or an erotic dream?

'Do you want to wait here or would you like to look around the plane?'

With a sigh she released her seat belt. 'I wouldn't mind stretching my legs.' A cold shower would have been better but she eagerly seized on the opportunity to not think about what had just happened. 'I suppose we should crack on.'

He looked at the nape of her neck and wondered how he had ever *not* seen past her disguise. He agreed in a colourless tone, 'By all means let us...*crack on.*'

It was predictably hot outside, but Tair appeared not to feel the heat as he led the way to his plane. Molly, trotting a few feet behind him, was uncomfortably conscious of the sweat breaking on her skin and by the time they got inside the plane everything was sticking in an unpleasant way.

Without a word Tair left her in the passenger section while he went towards the cockpit area, to retrieve whatever it was he had presumably taken the detour for.

'I'll just take a look around, shall I?' she called out. He ignored her. 'Rude rat,' she muttered, mentally conceding that he was a very sexy rude rat! She had never got the dark, smouldering, bad-boy thing before, but she was starting to see the appeal. Her eyes widened with horror at this realisation and she pressed her fist into her mouth to stop herself groaning out loud.

What was she doing?

Nothing, she hadn't done anything. *Yet*, said the voice in her head and she groaned again, pressing her arms to her stomach and rocking forward.

At the sound of the engine roaring into life she pulled upright and walked quickly towards the cockpit that was partitioned off from the rest of the plane by a curtain.

She pulled it back to reveal Tair sitting in the pilot's chair, clicking switches.

'I don't know if you've noticed,' she said, trying to sound casual, because she didn't want to come across as some sort of neurotic female, 'but we're moving.'

Not looking at her, he carried on clicking and consulting dials. 'Yes.'

'So is that normal?'

'When you're about to take off it is.'

'I thought for a second you said take off.'

He turned his head and flashed her a smile that sent a chill of apprehension through her. 'I did.'

She gave a shaky laugh. 'If you're trying to scare me, it worked.'

'Then I'm not trying, I'm succeeding.'

Molly gritted her teeth… Don't lose it, she told herself. 'Will you look at me?'

He did, but only for a split second. 'That might not be such a good idea just now.'

His sardonic tone brought a flush of anger to her pale face. 'What are you doing, Tair?'

'I could tell you but I think the technical detail might pass over your head.'

Molly felt as if her head were going to explode. 'It's insane, if you're doing what it looks like. Are you really…?'

'You should belt yourself in.'

Molly paled, her shaking hands reaching for the back of a seat as her mind started to spin. 'But surely you can stop it?' She felt stupid for asking, but she needed some reassurance and if he was coping with an emergency she probably ought not to ask such questions.

'I could,' he agreed. Molly barely had time to start relaxing when he flashed her a flat look and added after a pause. 'But I'm not going to.'

Presumably this was his idea of a joke. The alternative was not one she wanted to think about. She gave a laugh to show him he hadn't spooked her.

'And this is the moment I'm supposed to panic?' Pursing her lips, she shook her head slowly from side to side. 'Sorry, but I'm not falling for that one.'

He turned his head and looked at her just for a second, an arctic coldness in his azure eyes that appeared far too realistic to be part of any joke. His dark brows arched.

'Suit yourself.'

Molly's temper flared at the dismissal in his manner. 'Will you look at me when we're talking?' she yelled shrilly.

'You can talk, and you no doubt will—I've yet to meet a woman who understood the value of silence—but I'm busy flying a plane.'

She glared at the back of his neck in frustration. 'Will you stop saying that? You're *not* flying a plane!' The fear she was struggling to control sent her voice up a quivering octave.

'Well, if I'm not, who is? Sit down and belt yourself in. We're taking off. We can discuss this later.'

Molly abandoned reason. 'We can't…' She heard the throbbing note of rising panic in her voice and stopped to take a deep breath. 'Tair,' she said hoarsely. 'Please think for a moment about what you're doing.'

She had tried shrill demands and now she was resorting to husky seductiveness, Tair thought. He wondered if the husky little catch in her voice normally worked and decided if the damage it was doing to his concentration was any indicator it probably did.

'You're insane!'

Not that he looked it—in fact he was emanating a statuesque calm as he sat behind the control panel.

'I don't know why you're doing this. Maybe you have your reasons.' Most lunatics did. 'But it's nothing to do with me so why don't you stop the plane and let me off?' Preferably now before they were several thousand feet above the ground. The way the plane was picking up speed suggested that this moment was not far off.

He flashed her a contemptuous look. 'It has everything to do with you.'

'I don't know what you're talking about,' she said miserably. She shook her head slowly from side to side, baffled confusion in her pale face as she tensely grabbed hold of the back of his seat to steady herself and looked around the enclosed space like a hunted animal seeking an escape route.

'Look, nobody's going to hurt you.' While Tair was totally furious with her and felt nothing but utter contempt for her lack of morals and selfishness, he didn't get anything but an uneasy feeling from making a woman look petrified. 'Sit down, buckle up and shut up.'

Molly would have loved to tell him what he could do with his orders, but as the aircraft put on a final spurt of speed self-preservation seemed more of a priority.

Like an automaton she did what he had curtly ordered with the addition of closing her eyes.

* * *

'You can unfasten your seat belt now.'

Molly opened her eyes, but her white-knuckled fingers stayed tight around the metal clasp. They really were in the air!

'What are you doing?'

'Switching to autopilot.'

'No, I mean *what are you doing*?' Her voice rose to a shrill shriek.

'I would have thought that was obvious.'

Her mind still shied away from putting words to her situation. 'You're kidnapping me?' she said, hoping he'd laugh and say something cutting about how he could have any woman so why would he want to kidnap her.

He didn't laugh, he just said calmly, 'An emotive way of putting it, but I suppose essentially accurate. Though, like I said, you are not in danger. Nobody is going to harm you.'

'Are you mad?' A stupid question because if he was he would deny it. The mad people in films always thought they were sane.

'You can't go around kidnapping people.'

'I don't. This is a first.'

'I feel so special,' she inserted weakly. His mental health was no longer in question. 'Did you plan this or did you wake up this morning and think you might try abducting someone today?'

'As I said, you're not in any danger, so why not just sit back and enjoy the ride?'

Molly's chest swelled with indignation. 'Enjoy?' She took a deep breath and forced herself to smile, though the effect was slightly spoiled by the gold glow of fury in her eyes. 'Look, take me back and I won't say anything. I won't tell anyone,' she promised.

He looked at her with a chilling lack of emotion, and it was that that scared Molly more than anything yet.

'Do you dislike me so much?'

'This is not personal.' At least, it shouldn't be, thought

Tair. But as an inherently honest person, he recognised the moment he spoke that this was not so—he had a personal reaction to everything this woman did, including when she stared at him with big reproachful eyes. 'I have no feelings one way or the other about you,' he added with a contemptuous sneer that said otherwise.

Molly lifted a hand to her head. 'This is surreal. It can't be happening.'

'As I said, you might as well relax and enjoy the ride.'

'I'm not going to enjoy anything. I hate you—you're…' She stopped, sucking in a steadying breath while forcing her stiff features into a smile of appeal. 'Look, just turn this thing around. You can't do this! What about Beatrice? What will she think when we don't turn up at the hospital?'

If they taught duplicity she would be a straight-A student. Tair considered himself a pretty good judge of character, but even when he looked in her eyes all he saw was genuine anxiety for a friend.

He saw different things when he looked at her mouth, so it was probably better not to go there, he thought. It was a pity his cousin had not displayed a similar amount of self-control where the Mouse's mouth was concerned, he reflected, his jaw hardening.

'I imagine that Beatrice will feel relief if she's got the faintest idea about what you're up to.'

'What are you talking about? Beatrice will be worried sick.'

He turned in his seat, his eyes like ice chips. 'Enough!'

Molly flinched at the staccato command and drew back in her own seat. His blazing blue eyes raked her face.

'You should know, Miss Mouse, that I have zero tolerance with liars and cheats, so no more of this nauseating pretence of concern.'

Molly shook her head in utter confusion.

Tair watched as she gave a brilliant performance of being scared and even though he knew it was fake he still felt like a total brute.

'Stop acting!'

'I'm not.'

His lips curled expressively. 'I doubt that a woman like you knows the meaning of the word care. How could you when you pretend to be Beatrice's friend and all the time you're seducing her husband?'

Her jaw dropped. 'I've never seduced anyone in my life. I wouldn't know where to begin.'

She forced her next words past the wild hysterical laugh that was locked in her throat. 'You think I'm having an affair with Tariq…?'

'There are others? You are a serial seductress?'

She ignored the acid insert and carried on staring at him blankly. She wiped the moisture from her eyes, the tears having been an emotional release of a sort—at last she finally knew what this was about. 'You have no idea.'

She had no idea how badly he wanted to cover her mouth with his, Tair thought, or she might not look so relaxed.

'Is anything about you the real thing?' His lip curled in disgust. 'There's nothing about you to alarm a wife, is there, with your meek mouse look and the ridiculous glasses you don't need?'

Molly wiped away the tears from her cheeks and hastened to set the record straight. 'I can't help my face and there's nothing sinister about my glasses. They're just…I wanted to look older and it got to be a habit…'

Her voice trailed away as she recognised that even to her ears this explanation sounded weak. So much for honesty being the best policy!

Her present predicament was a perfect example of how in the

real world a lie frequently sounded more credible than the truth. Laughter would be the most likely response she'd get if she went around telling her family and friends an Arab prince had kidnapped her because he thought she was some sort of... How on earth *had* he decided she was some sort of *femme fatale*?

'I'm flattered you think I'm so irresistible, but—'

'I am not such an easy mark as my cousin, Miss Mouse.' His voice dropped to a nerve-tingling purr as he added softly, 'I prefer to be the hunter and not the hunted.'

Looking at his dark, proud, predatory features, Molly did not find this statement hard to believe. 'That was a joke,' she said hoarsely. 'This isn't what you think...'

A look of bored irritation, slightly marred by the nerve that clenched and unclenched in his lean cheek, settled on his handsome face. 'Before you launch into an impassioned and lengthy speech of denial, let me explain that I saw Tariq coming out of your room last night.'

'Last night...' Her eyes widened. 'Oh, last night, but that was...' She stopped, her soft features stretching into a grimace as she recalled her promise to Tariq.

'Perfectly innocent?'

The sarcasm brought an angry tide of colour to her cheeks. 'As a matter of fact it was.'

'The sad thing is that Beatrice is probably trying to tell herself the same thing.'

Molly's eyes locked with his contemptuous gaze as she struggled to follow. 'Should I understand what you're trying to say?' It seemed safe to assume there was an insult in there somewhere.

If she had shown a flicker of remorse and not maintained this ridiculous denial he might have felt more inclined to show some tolerance. Weakness was forgivable, but her calculated selfish attitude was not.

'If you had an ounce of empathy you might. But you are

clearly incapable of putting yourself in anyone's skin but your own.' As his scornful gaze drifted down the pale column of her throat he was forced to concede that it was pretty perfect skin, pale and flawless with a glow he might have imagined was an outward sign of inner radiance had he not known what a selfish little cheat she actually was.

'Whereas you are totally able to identify with a wronged wife? Or is it just Bea that has a special place in your heart?'

He sucked in an angry breath through flared nostrils. 'Be very careful what you say, Miss Mouse.'

Molly tossed her head, but beneath her defiance she was actually nervous. Tair Al Sharif was a dangerous man and she was making him very angry. The problem was she couldn't seem to stop herself.

After a lifetime of caution and prudence she was suddenly acting with a reckless lack of restraint and a part of her was actually enjoying it! It was almost liberating, she thought, before also thinking that she must be deeply twisted to feel that way.

'Well, you do seem very concerned about Beatrice.' She hoped that he couldn't hear the undercurrent of unattractive jealousy that made her inwardly wince. 'Maybe,' she speculated, 'you're projecting your guilt onto me because you think I'm doing what you'd secretly like to. Or maybe you're a hypocrite and have already done it?'

She knew she'd gone too far the moment the provocative jibe left her lips, but, unable to back down, she lifted her chin and watched the dull colour run up under his golden skin.

If someone had offered her a million pounds to take her eyes off his face it wouldn't have made any difference—there was something totally compelling about the fury etched in the powerful lines and sharp angles of his overwhelmingly masculine features.

Her defiant façade wobbled as his anger hit her like a solid wall. She swallowed as she lifted a shaking hand to her throat, where a pulse ticked like a time bomb.

'Is someone flying this plane?' she asked, hoping to divert him. 'I suppose,' she added nervously, 'that you can multitask.' As in throttle her while flying a small plane across the desert.

'I would *never* creep around and have some sordid affair!' He didn't raise his voice but Tair managed to pack enough menace in his soft words to scare the life out of anyone with an ounce of self-preservation. 'Do not judge others by your own gutter standards.'

His contempt caught Molly on the raw. How dared he take the high moral ground? She was pretty sure he had more skeletons in his cupboard than she did—she didn't have any, which made her incredibly boring.

In some ways, she mused, it was almost better to be thought a bitch than boring.

'Have I got this right?' she said, adopting an expression of exaggerated bemusement. 'It's not that you wouldn't like to have an affair, it's just that you're too pure, too good to have an affair?'

'I do not pretend to be a saint—'

With a mouth like his—a mouth that invited sinful thoughts—it would have been pretty pointless, she thought, her eyes lingering on the firm sensual curve.

'I would never have an affair,' he repeated in a goaded voice. 'Because I saw firsthand what my father's affairs did to my mother. He never tried to hide them, he actually seemed to take a malicious pleasure in humiliating her, parading his women in front of her. She was a proud woman but he wore away her spirit and her pride.'

Tair thought how his mother would be little more than a memory to him had it not been for the diaries her maid had given him when he was sixteen. Those diaries had provided some insight into how a woman who was humiliated by her husband's repeated infidelities might feel.

Tair Al Sharif was the last man on the planet Molly had ever expected to feel any empathy for, but as she watched him close his eyes and drag a hand through his dark hair her heart ached for him.

To watch one parent do that to another and be unable to do a thing but stand and watch must be terrible for any child. The king sounded like a vile man. He might not have actually raised his hand to his wife, but his actions were another equally damaging form of abuse.

Molly voiced her next thought without realising. 'He must have loved her once.' Although she couldn't understand how anyone could do that to another person, let alone someone they had ever cared for.

At the sound of her voice Tair's head lifted and he looked straight into amber eyes glowing with the compassion he'd accused her of not possessing.

He bit back a curse. He had broken the habit of a lifetime by allowing her to goad him into justifying himself and as a direct result he had got sucked into a conversation that touched on deeply personal issues. Issues he would not have chosen to discuss with his closest friends.

'It was my father's second marriage, a political arrangement not a love match.'

He spoke in a manner designed to close the subject and make it quite clear he didn't require her understanding.

Any more than he required Molly James's good opinion.

'To force someone into a loveless marriage is so callous and cruel!' she exclaimed.

Clearly she had not received the message.

'Possibly,' he conceded in his most chilling voice. 'But,

please, no more of the slushy sentimentality. I have a weak stomach.'

And, it would seem, an allergy to sympathy. She had never seen him look so uncomfortable. He obviously didn't want anyone to suspect he had any weak spots.

'Relax,' she drawled.

He shook his head in irritated incomprehension. 'I beg your pardon?'

'I'm not going to feel sorry for you—if it makes you feel any better I still can't stand the sight of you!'

It might have been her imagination but the glimmer in his eyes might have been humour. 'Or I you.'

'And I'm allowed an opinion.'

His brows lifted. 'One?'

'I still think arranged marriages are totally wrong.'

'Not all arranged marriages are unhappy and there is no force involved in such arrangements. Many arranged marriages are successful. Sometimes they are necessary. A person cannot always put their happiness ahead of their duty.'

She not only didn't look convinced, she looked appalled. Her eyes suddenly widened. 'Would you…?'

'I am the heir, and political alliances are important.' He consulted the dials, made a quick mental calculation and nodded before turning back to her.

'But surely seeing how unhappy a marriage like that made your mother…'

'Many love matches do not end in undiluted joy… Tariq professed to love Beatrice.'

A flash of anger lit Molly's eyes. 'You're not comparing Tariq with someone like your father?'

'No, I'm not, but you're a lot more dangerous, Miss Mouse, than my father's mistresses.'

The novelty of being called dangerous momentarily robbed her of speech.

'With them what you saw was what you got. They were not exactly subtle.' His lips thinned with contempt. 'You're insidious, you creep up on a man and because you seem so benign and harmless there are no alarm bells, a man doesn't realise you've crept under his skin and your voice has seeped into his bloodstream until it's happened.' He reached out and touched a strand of the shiny hair that had escaped its confinement. 'There's something about you that takes a man over the edge.'

Her insides trembled as his fingertips grazed her cheek before his hand fell away. His shoulders lifted in a fluid shrug while his eyes drifted across her flushed features. 'With temptation out of the way—' his eyes slid to her mouth and he thought how that sort of temptation did not come more appealingly packaged '—I don't think it will take Tariq long to remember where his loyalties lie. For him to realise that Beatrice is worth ten of a woman like you!'

CHAPTER FIVE

IT WAS so mind-bogglingly weird to have a man who looked like Tair talking as though she were some sort of sexy siren that if Molly hadn't been so furious she might have been flattered.

'Temptresses don't wear B-cup bras.'

His blue gaze fell to her chest and stayed there.

Painfully conscious of her tingling nipples, she clenched her fists to stop herself covering them. 'And if,' she continued hoarsely, 'I *was* having an affair…'

This brought his eyes upwards and she saw there was a cynical gleam in his sky-blue beautiful gaze. 'So you admit it.'

She ground her teeth. 'I've never been a swearing sort of person but I'm starting to feel I could learn fast. How can I spell it out so that even you can understand? I am not having an affair with anyone.

'But,' she added, miming a zipping motion across her lips to forestall the inevitable sarcastic intervention from him. She was guessing from the look of sheer stunned incredulity on his hatefully perfect face that he didn't get told to shut up even in sign language very often.

'Even if I was, what gives you the right to interfere in other people's lives?' Given the fact she was going to have to break her promise to Tariq, because nothing but the truth was going to stop this man going through with his crazy plan, she felt she had the right to demand a few explanations from Tair Al Sharif first!

She gritted her teeth, resenting the fact that she was left with little choice but to expose her connection with the Al Kamal Royal household. She watched as he fixed her with a contemptuous stare.

It was so unfair, she thought, eying him with simmering resentment. The man couldn't look anything less than in-credible even if he tried. His hair probably looked sexily rumpled when he woke in the morning. Her eyes narrowed as the mental picture of him in bed first thing grew in her head. The dark shadow on his jaw…the sleepy sex look in his heavy-lidded eyes…?

She stopped and moved her hand in a sweeping motion in front of her face in an effort to make the image disappear. It could not be healthy or wise to spend time wondering about how a man who had just kidnapped her would look after a night of passion. This was something someone who had just been kidnapped should definitely not want to know. Though this didn't seem to stop her eyes from being drawn to the firm contours of his sculpted lips and a little shiver shimmying up her spine as she considered how he would hardly be a low-maintenance lover.

As if she knew much about lovers.

She ignored the voice in her head and the little bubble of excitement that exploded in her belly like a hot star-burst as Tair answered her question.

'You mean I should cross to the metaphorical other side of the street and watch my friends' marriage destroyed? Which wouldn't, if last night was anything to go by, be very long. How long do you think it would have been before people caught on? I mean, you were hardly very discreet—all those yearning looks and meaningful glances across the table.'

'Not everyone has a mind like a sewer. This is so stupid!' she wailed. 'Why couldn't you just have minded your own business? But I forgot—everything *is* your business,' she added bitterly.

Her insults slid off him like water off a duck's back.

Molly sucked in an angry breath through flared nostrils and glared at the back of his neck. 'Will you look at me when I'm talking to you? Not only are you a control freak, you're a control freak with no manners.'

'You can have manners or you can arrive alive—take your pick. There is some turbulence ahead that requires my attention.' As if to back up this point the small plane took a sudden unscheduled drop. 'Fasten your seat belt.'

Molly was already buckling up.

The pocket of turbulence lasted another few minutes, but it seemed longer to Molly, who was not a good flyer at the best of times.

She expelled a long shaky sigh when Tair removed his brown fingers from the controls and struggled to match his nonchalant attitude to the white-knuckle ride they had just endured.

'You were saying?' He did not pause to allow her to respond but added, 'Let me help you—you were explaining that I am a control freak with no manners. You might incidentally like to keep such opinions to yourself when we are not alone as it is not exactly customary to speak to me this way.'

'You think you're so clever, don't you? If you were half as omnipotent as you like to think…' She squeezed her eyes tight shut and *just* managed to stop herself blurting out the truth. She wanted to choose her moment and watch this man's ego deflate when he realised his mistake.

'Your arrogance really is off the scale, you know. How would you like it if Tariq interfered in your love affairs?'

He wouldn't like it all, but to Tair's way of thinking that was not the point.

'I interfere because I can and because seeing them together gives hope to the rest of us…' He stopped, perturbed that he had allowed her to goad him into the admission, an admission he had not previously acknowledged even to himself.

The utterly unexpected response made Molly, who was mentally rehearsing her speech about how Tariq and Khalid were her half-brothers, lose her thread. 'You envy what they have?'

Envy implied he wanted what they had, and he was the last person in the world who she would have thought craved love and babies.

'There is very little point envying what you cannot have.'

She struggled to hide her curiosity and failed. 'Why can't you have it?'

His eyes narrowed. 'Why can't you stop talking?' he cut back sharply. He did not care for Miss Mouse applying her amateur psychology to him.

'Possibly it is a reaction to being kidnapped. You haven't thought this through. What do you think's going to happen? I can't just vanish off the face of the earth?'

He gave a scornful snort. 'You are so important?'

'Not like you maybe,' she snapped sarcastically. 'People don't bow to my every wish, but I hope you realise they do that out of fear, not respect.'

'Actually it is tradition.' It was a tradition he would happily have consigned to history, but such changes were not brought about overnight.

Her expression showed what she thought of tradition, but, in case he didn't get the message, she added with a sneer, 'I'd *die* before I bow to you!'

He threw back his head and laughed. The deep, uninhibited sound was attractive. Unlike his personality, she muttered under her breath.

'Bowing is not essential to my plan. You really do have a turn for the dramatic. That is something I had not anticipated,' he admitted, his glance moving from her sparkling eyes and flushed cheeks to her heaving bosom. Neither had he anticipated feeling attracted to her this way.

Her cheeks flamed. 'You think *that's* dramatic,' she said, tossing her head and waving her finger at him.

He pursed his lips and let out a silent whistle. 'My, you do have a temper.'

'It's not the only thing I have. I have people who care about me,' she told him in a voice that shook. 'My half-brothers…actually, you know—' She stopped abruptly mid-tirade and gasped. 'Oh, my God!'

Tair watched as the colour drained from her skin, leaving her paper-pale.

'Dad,' she whispered in a stricken voice, her eyes widening in horror.

'Your father?'

She nodded. 'My dad has a heart condition. He's waiting for bypass surgery—if he finds out I've gone missing it will kill him.'

'Of course it will.'

She looked at him in total disgust. 'You callous bastard!'

He gave a fluid shrug. 'Possibly, but not a gullible one, though I have to admit you are good. Have you thought about writing fiction?'

'But it's true!' she protested, tears of frustration standing out in her eyes as she struggled to convince him of her sincerity.

'Dad had his first heart attack when he was forty! Then last week—' She stopped and gulped as the memory of that phone conversation the previous week came rushing back.

A conversation that had begun with the words 'Don't panic but' had never been one she was going to enjoy.

She hadn't.

Molly had listened with a knot of apprehension like a boulder lodged behind her breastbone as her dad had explained that he'd had a few twinges recently.

'Define twinges or, better still, get the doctor to define them. You have to promise me to make an appointment right now.'

'No need. Actually I was out cycling the tow-path the other day and I had a slightly bigger twinge and a chap passing by called an ambulance.'

'You mean you had a heart attack.' By this point Molly was already mentally booking her flight home.

'Not a heart attack, just angina.'

'Just angina?' she echoed, wanting to scream with sheer frustration. 'Oh, well, that's all right, then.'

His sigh vibrated gently down the line. 'I told your sisters you'd react this way but they made me ring you.'

'I'm coming home right now.'

'Look, Molly, there is absolutely no point you coming home now. They won't be doing the bypass until next month or most probably the month after—the waiting list is huge.'

Molly, who had been pacing the room, sat down with a bump. 'You need a bypass?'

'Didn't I say?'

'Well, heart surgery is something that could slip a person's mind, isn't it, Dad?' she said bitterly. 'You're impossible!' And the possibility of not having her impossible parent around to drive her crazy filled her with gut-churning terror. 'I'm coming home.'

'The doctors have told me to avoid stress and if you come home now because of me I'm going to feel stressed.'

Molly hadn't been convinced by this argument, but after she had spoken to her sisters she had realised there was a grain of truth in it. Now she knew it was the biggest mistake of her life. If she had gone home when she should have she wouldn't now be in a plane with a certifiable lunatic.

She took a deep breath and reached out, her fingers curling around Tair's forearm as she levelled her gaze with his. 'Look,' she said, pointing at her face. 'Do I look as though I'm lying?'

He looked bored and said, 'This is old ground.'

'You don't understand. If my father hears about this…' She clamped her quivering lips tight as she added in a fearful whisper, 'It will kill him. He needs heart surgery, you see—he's not supposed to be stressed.'

'That is very inventive.'

Her fists balled in frustration. 'It's not an invention, it's the truth.'

His lip curled. 'Do I look like a gullible idiot?'

'Look…I'm wasting my breath, aren't I?' She fixed him with a glare of sheer loathing as she added, 'If anything happens to my father you'll be responsible and I'll make you pay if it's the last thing I do.'

She turned her head sharply so that he couldn't see the tears that welled up in her eyes, and she missed the flash of uncertainty in his face.

'There are not going to be any alarm bells ringing to alert your father. You haven't vanished. Being a considerate friend you have decided not to impose on Beatrice's hospitality at a moment that is essentially a family time. You left a note.'

Molly closed her eyes. She could only imagine Tariq's face when he read that note. A laugh escaped her dry lips.

'You're not going to have hysterics again, are you?'

Molly just stared. 'Won't they think it odd that I didn't write personally?'

'You're avoiding an embarrassing scene.'

'But why in this alternative universe am I embarrassed?'

'You have accepted an invitation from a man you have just met…' He stopped as the gulping sound of a strangled sob escaped her throat.

He looked at the tears sliding down her cheeks and was irritated to feel an irrational stab of guilt. This woman is a born manipulator, he reminded himself.

'Do you actually have a father?' he wondered harshly.

'I do and I also have brothers…Tariq…'

'Is your brother, I suppose?' he drawled.

Molly's shoulders relaxed. 'Yes…but it isn't public knowledge and I'd prefer it stayed that way.'

'I imagine you would.' He smirked as he scanned her face. 'I'm disappointed,' he admitted.

'Disappointed?' she echoed, wishing she'd come clean straight off and avoided this journey. 'Don't worry, I won't start some sort of diplomatic incident by telling everyone about this.'

'Disappointed,' he corrected, 'because I had thought your powers of invention were limitless, but apparently not. Let me offer you a word of advice. The thing about lies is that one needs to keep them this side of reality. The "seriously ill father" story was far more convincing.'

Her horrified eyes flew to his face. He thought she was lying.

'He is!' Even as she spoke she knew that there was not a chance in hell of convincing him. It was all about timing and hers stunk!

She shook her head and narrowed her eyes. 'Tariq is my brother and he will come looking for me…and then you'll be sorry,' she promised, sheer will-power holding back the tears that threatened to fall from her glistening eyes.

His lip curled. 'I think you overestimate your value to Tariq. As far as he is concerned you got a better offer and are with me.'

'He will come,' she said, fixing him a glare of complete loathing.

'I can't decide if you actually imagine you're in love with Tariq or if it was a harmless flirtation that went too far, and quite frankly your motivation doesn't interest me.'

Despite this declaration of disinterest he immediately began to speculate. 'Is this pay-back time for all the years you must have stood in Beatrice's shadow? It must have been frustrating—with Beatrice around nobody was going to look at you, were they?' His burning blue eyes slid with dismissive contempt over her slender body.

'Who could blame you,' he continued, 'for being tempted when the opportunity arose? Someone was looking at you, not Beatrice.'

'You seem to be managing it.'

The observation brought a flash of anger to his lean face. 'Did it not even occur to you that you were hurting people?'

'Did it occur to you that you're wrong?'

CHAPTER SIX

'SILLY question, of course it didn't. But you are wrong about everything. Tariq will come and when he does you won't look so smug and self-satisfied.'

It was hard to tell how long the uneasy, hostile silence had lasted before Tair finally raised his voice and called out.

'Fasten your belt—we're going to land.'

Molly, who had taken a seat in the rear of the plane as far away from him as possible, did as he requested. Rebellion for rebellion's sake was not going to achieve anything. She had to plan her strategy and in the meantime she could only hope that her brothers would have the sense to shelter her dad from the truth for as long as possible.

'It might be a little rough.'

Molly considered this an understatement, but when she looked out of the window and saw where they had landed she was amazed that they were still in one piece.

It was, quite literally, the middle of nowhere.

Her plans of being noisy and hoping someone would rescue her disintegrated. He sauntered down the plane looking so relaxed that she felt like screaming in frustration.

She resisted the temptation, realising her best bet was to lull him into a false sense of security by letting him think he was in charge, and that she was beaten.

He's not? You're not? she wondered.

'Right, I am glad you are being sensible.'

Carry on believing that, you rat, she thought, catching the piece of white garment he threw at her.

'Put it on.'

Without waiting to see if she did, obviously taking obedience as a given, he turned and walked back to the cockpit. When he returned a short time later his hair was concealed in a traditional white desert headdress, and Molly felt a quiver run down her spine. The covering emphasised the perfect bone structure and hard sculpted contours of his sternly beautiful face.

It also revealed the primitive quality that she found disturbingly compelling. The veneer of civilisation he cloaked himself in was paper-thin as he looked at her.

'Are you ready?'

Tair watched as she removed her hands from the armrests without saying a word. Fingers stiff, she unfastened the clasp of her belt and got to her feet.

Though she purposefully did not look at him, Molly was very conscious of his brooding presence towering over her. She lifted her lashes and when she saw his face again she lost her balance. As she took a staggering step back he reached out and grabbed her while saying something harsh-sounding in his own tongue.

A second later the breath left her lungs in a soft whoosh as she was brought into direct contact with the iron-hard surface of his chest.

'Are you all right?' he asked again.

Molly struggled to catch her breath and fought even harder against the paralysis that caused her to lean into him, not because she had to, but because she wanted to.

Now that was scary!

One of his arms was wrapped around her ribs, but not so

tightly as to confine her. It was her own starved senses that held her there as she drank in the male fragrance of his warm body.

Taking a deep breath, she managed to gain enough control to push away. His hands went to her shoulders and stayed there.

'Are you sure you're all right?' he asked again.

Molly nodded, feeling uncomfortably exposed as his blue eyes scanned her face. Glaring up at him, she breathed hard to drag air into her lungs.

'Let me tell you what will happen next.'

'I already know what will happen next,' she snapped, twisting away from him. The sound of his grunt of pain as her wild kick made contact with the most vulnerable part of his anatomy, delivered more by luck than skill, gave her a surge of satisfaction as, yelling at the top of her lungs, she flung herself towards the door.

She had not reached the opening before a hand looped around her waist. Her feet left the floor as she was pulled back against his hard physique. An adrenaline rush gave her strength and fear fuelled her desperation as she flailed out at him, her fists hammering into his chest. She was literally sobbing in frustration as he restrained her with insulting ease.

'Let me go, you… Help!'

'Nobody can hear you.' Through her pants of exertion his voice sounded calm. 'I don't want to hurt you, but that doesn't mean I won't.'

'My,' she sneered. 'Aren't you the big man?'

'Aren't you the little wild cat?' he countered, looking at her with an expression that made her stomach flip. The fight drained out of her quite abruptly and if he hadn't been holding her she would have slid to the floor. 'Do not waste your energy.'

What energy? she thought, suddenly feeling as weak as a kitten and a harsh word away from humiliating tears.

'There is no one to hear you and nowhere to run. Do you understand?'

She nodded and he released her. Molly pushed a hank of hair from her face with her forearm—the last of her hair pins had been lost some time earlier—and fixed him with a steady unblinking regard.

'I hate you,' she announced shakily but with conviction, her golden eyes filled with loathing.

'I'm not exactly a fan of yours either. You kick like a mule. Remind me not to leave any sharp implements around.'

He picked up the white cotton garment from the floor. 'Now put it on.'

His lips tightened as she shook her head. 'It's just the sort of thing you like—baggy and shapeless. It will also protect you from the sun; it's another two hours before dusk.'

'Where are you taking me?'

'Somewhere where you can't do any harm,' he said, and then, because he could see the next question and didn't want to hear her voice again, added, 'My grandfather has an encampment a few kilometres from here.'

She sniffed and tossed her head, starting off a rippling motion in her loose hair before it settled straight and smooth down her back. 'So this abduction is a family business, is it? Your grandfather must be so proud of you.'

Tair watched her hair and thought about how it would feel brushing against his skin. Not that he intended finding out, but a man couldn't help but wonder.

'My grandfather won't be there.' His lips curved into an ironic smile as he imagined his grandfather's response to him turning up with a golden-eyed captive in tow. Explosive would hardly cover it!

His smile faded abruptly. His grandfather's reaction would not be any stronger than the desire that had exploded inside him when he had held Molly's soft and trembling body in his arms. He had wanted to both comfort her and taste her—neither of which were appropriate responses.

'He is attending a gathering…a race meeting.'

'Horse racing in the desert?'

'Camel.'

'You race camels?'

'It is tradition. The location varies but there is a large gathering every year.'

'And when you don't turn up?'

'I will.' He would regain a little perspective once there was a safe distance between them.

Molly couldn't hide her surprise—although shouldn't it be relief? 'So you're not staying with me.'

One corner of his mouth lifted in a taunting smile. 'Will you miss me?'

The hot colour flew to her cheeks. 'About as much as the flu.'

He laughed. 'Come on—your carriage awaits.'

Only it wasn't a carriage.

A few minutes later she stood looking at two camels, shaking her head. 'You have to be joking?'

He didn't respond, though he did crack a grin once or twice when she was attempting to get onto her camel with the assistance of one of the two men who had met them.

'This animal smells disgusting.'

'He probably thinks the same about you,' he retorted, thinking not for the first time about the scent that clung to her hair.

She folded her arms and shook her head. 'I can't.'

'Show a bit of backbone. It's just like sitting in an armchair.'

'Show a bit of backbone?' she repeated, her voice rising an indignant octave. 'I'd like to see how much backbone you'd be showing if the roles were reversed. I've been kidnapped, verbally abused, starved and now you expect me to ride a damn camel. Well, enough is enough!' she said, sinking to the floor and proceeding to sit cross-legged.

The two men looked to Tair, who said something in Arabic that made them smile.

'What did you say to them about me?'

'I said that normally you have the sweet nature of a dove, but you're having a bad day.'

She threw him an acid look, then let out a shriek when one of the men picked her up, put her on the camel, then urged the animal forward.

'You're doing very well.'

'Save your words of encouragement. If I fall off and break my neck you'll have it on your conscience for ever.'

'You won't fall off—you're a natural.'

She grunted something indistinct and slung him a murderous glare. He grinned and urged his own mount ahead, leaving her precious little choice but to follow. She didn't know where they were or where they were going to. All around was an undulating vast expanse of nothingness.

Either the camels knew their way home or Tair was one of those people who possessed an inbuilt compass.

It was dusk when they reached the top of a rise and saw the encampment spread below them.

Molly caught her breath—it was amazing!

The clusters of tents were pitched around what must be an area that possessed a natural water supply, because as well as the palm trees swaying overhead she could hear the faint but distinctive sound of falling water above the buzz of people moving about their business. Fires had been lit, sending sparks into the velvet smoke-filled evening air.

Despite the fact she was hot, tired, uncomfortable and mad as hell, Molly was enchanted by the scene.

'It's beautiful.' Aware of Tair's eyes on her face, she added tetchily, 'I don't suppose anyone here is going to help me if I tell them you've kidnapped me?'

'Are you sure you want them to listen?'

Molly's cheeks scored with angry colour as she turned her head and nearly lost her balance in the process. 'Are you suggesting that I like being forced to endure your company and your insults just because you have a pretty face?'

She knew straight away that her words were a mistake and the speculative gleam that entered his eyes confirmed this.

'I wasn't thinking of my face particularly, I've never been called pretty before, but I'm naturally relieved that it meets with your approval, Miss Mouse.'

Molly gritted her teeth and refused to respond to the taunt.

'I was thinking that if I didn't know better...' His dark head, tilted a little to one side, subjected her face to a narrowed-eyed scrutiny until Molly could bear it no longer and snapped.

'If you didn't know better what?'

'If I didn't know better I'd say that you were enjoying your adventure.'

Her rebuttal to this crazy contention was instant and robust. 'And if you did say that I'd say you were insane.'

Tair didn't respond, but instead gave a shrug and tapped her mount sharply on the rump to get it moving.

What did he think she was? she wondered as she watched him ride ahead. Some sort of adrenaline junkie? Adventure indeed!

She loosed a scornful laugh at the notion. All the same there had been a few moments...

Moments of what, Molly—terror?

Dismissing the creeping doubts in her head, she clung on as her mount surged forwards, responding perhaps to the noise of greeting as Tair reached the camp.

* * *

It quickly became clear that they were expected. She watched from a distance as people gathered around Tair, their attitude welcoming but respectful.

She closed her eyes and held tight as her camel responded to a command from someone and lurched to the ground for her to dismount.

As Molly turned her head to thank the man who helped her extricate her stiff and aching body from the saddle her face dropped.

Unless it was his twin, it was the same man who had helped her into the saddle two hours earlier…two sweltering, gruelling and bottom-numbing hours earlier. Molly suspected that shortly she would be wishing she were still numb.

The next thing she saw was a four-wheel drive, solidifying her horrid suspicion. Tair was an utterly awful man. Picking up the overlong skirts of the white desert dress she wore, she stalked towards the distinctive tall figure of her persecutor.

'You did that on purpose, didn't you?' Voice quivering with outrage, she stabbed an accusing finger in Tair's direction. 'And don't,' she warned darkly, 'tell me you don't know what I'm talking about.'

She was vaguely conscious of the buzz of noise dying away, of people staring and parting like the sea as she took several more slightly unsteady steps towards Tair, who didn't even have the decency to show a scrap of remorse.

'They, those men…'

He folded his arms across his chest and inserted helpfully. 'Ahmed and Samir.'

Her teeth clenched. 'Ahmed and Samir travelled here in that car, and we could have too.'

He did not deny it and his provocative smile threw fuel on Molly's smouldering temper.

'But then you would have missed out on an experience that so few have firsthand.'

'For the very good reason that as a mode of transport those camels leave a lot to be desired.' She rubbed her bottom with feeling. 'They are in fact vile, smelly beasts, though not,' she added with another vicious jab in his direction, 'as vile as you!'

Her glance slid towards the dusty vehicle and her expression grew wistful. 'I bet it's air-conditioned too. I probably have prickly heat.' She passed a hand across the overheated skin of her face and her fingers came away covered in grit and dust.

'I suppose this is your warped idea of getting back at me for my imaginary sins?' Thinking how she was taking the punishment without having enjoyed the pleasure.

The humour died from his face as his lips thinned into a contemptuous line. 'This is mild compared with what some of my ancestors' ideas of punishment would be for a woman like you.'

'You know nothing about women like me because when women like me see someone who shares your gene pool coming their way they cross the road. My God, when you topple off your high tower of comfortable smug superiority I really want to be there to see it.'

Right now she wasn't seeing anything much. The rash of red dots that had started dancing across her vision midway through her tirade of abuse had been replaced by a blackness that was closing in like a blanket.

She could see Tair, stern and contemptuous and so beautiful part of her wanted to weep; she could see his lips moving but she couldn't hear what he was saying. The only thing Molly could hear was a loud whooshing noise like a train in a tunnel.

The last she knew was that the floor was coming up to meet her very fast.

CHAPTER SEVEN

MOLLY opened her eyes and blinked in a dazed fashion. She was in a room with a high ceiling that appeared to be made of billowing silk. It was really very pretty.

She inhaled and her nostrils twitched. The air was filled with a faint spicy scent, an elusive mixture of incense and cinnamon. She turned her head towards the light breeze that made the glass lanterns hanging above her sway slightly, but could not see beyond the carved screen that stood there, filled with sconces that held flickering candles.

'You're awake.'

Oh, God!

She closed her eyes again and grunted. 'I wish I wasn't.' Suddenly it all came flooding back, the events of the last twelve hours.

She stared at her bare feet protruding from beneath a thin sheet that was covering her and didn't connect the groan she heard with herself. She wriggled her toes. Someone had taken off her shoes before placing her on what seemed to be a low divan.

'My head hurts.' Molly narrowed her eyes against the light from the overhead lanterns, which was being reflected in the surface of a large ornate mirror to her right. As was her face.

She looked like a ghost, almost as pale as the compress laid across her forehead.

She removed it and let it fall to the ground from lax fingers.

The memory of how close she had been to hitting the hard ground head first before he'd caught her flashed vividly into Tair's mind, and his jaw tightened.

'That's because you're an idiot.'

An idiot, but also a woman.

A woman who had endured a day that would have physically and mentally taxed many men.

There had been a moment when he had held her seemingly lifeless body in his arms that he had thought… He swallowed as he pushed aside that memory.

He could rationalise his actions, but he knew that nothing she had done made him any less culpable for her collapse. He had been too full of self-righteous, crusading anger to take any account of her physical fragility when he had forced her to trek across the desert.

'Don't hold back, just tell it the way it is,' Molly drawled, raising herself on one elbow and squinting up at Tair, who had moved into her line of vision and was standing by her bed.

Her eyes had to go a long way up to reach his face.

Her stomach flipped. It was not the prince with the urbane charm and diplomatic manners and designer suit who stood there.

This man had a combustible edgy quality, as if, she mused, studying his strongly carved bronzed features, he was able to shed the thin veneer of civilisation in these surroundings and be himself.

'So this is my fault. Why am I not surprised?' she croaked… God, but her throat hurt, and why couldn't she stop staring like a kid pressing her nose against a sweet-shop window? 'I'm always amazed,' she said bitterly, 'at your ability to turn things around so that it's down to me that you're a total bastard with a vicious streak.'

Tair said something low and angry-sounding in his own language, then dragged a hand through his jet-black hair. 'I am aware that I am responsible.'

Molly grew wary as there was nothing to read in his stiff expression. He was admitting responsibility but not, as far as she could tell, any remorse.

'So you're going to let me go back home?'

'We will discuss that tomorrow.'

'You're just saying that to shut me up.'

'If I wanted to shut you up there are much more efficient ways I could do so!'

'I can imagine.'

Actually he doubted she could, but Tair was actively imagining ways in which her voice would be effectively stifled.

Even Miss Mouse might find it hard to talk when she was being kissed... He stared at her mouth and thought about how she would taste, the warmth of her lips and the sweet moisture of her mouth.

'Why are you staring at me like that?'

Tair gave himself a mental jolt and smoothly picked up the thread, saying, 'You want to discuss this? Fine—let's discuss how I repeatedly told you to take on fluids during the ride and you chose not to. You were dehydrated—that's why you passed out.'

Molly looked at him, wondering about the emotion she had briefly glimpsed on his face. But now he was looking at her through the screen of his dark lashes that were so long they brushed the slashing angle of his razor-edged cheekbones and she couldn't decide if she had imagined it or not.

'I never faint.'

There were big shadows under her eyes, she was the colour

of paper and, having suffered the after-effects of dehydration himself, he knew she must be feeling like hell, but still she came out fighting.

He wondered that he had ever thought her mousy and timid.

'And I never look after stupid, half-dead women, but there is a first time for everything.'

She looked at the glass he held out to her and shook her head. 'I'm not thirsty.'

He moved impatiently, causing the ice to clink against the sides. 'Do I look like I care?'

She accepted the invitation to study his face. He didn't appear to care one bit, but he did look like someone capable of pouring the contents of the glass down her throat if she didn't co-operate.

He also looked everything a woman could wish for in her wildest dreams. Lean, dark and brooding with an edge of danger. Normally Molly's dreams were much more sedate but as she gazed at him her heartbeat did quicken perceptibly as the silence stretched.

'Fine!' With an ungracious sniff she snatched the glass from his hand and lifted it to her lips.

'All of it.'

Molly narrowed her eyes. 'I…'

He silenced her with a look and, sighing, she did as he requested. 'Satisfied?' she asked, flopping back on the pillows. Her head was pounding. So was her heart, but, she recognised, not necessarily from the same cause.

'Not really. I hate stupidity, so why did you tell me you had drunk on our journey when I asked? I told—'

'And I told you to go to hell but you didn't,' she inserted childishly. 'And I did drink.'

He arched a sardonic brow and produced a water bottle from somewhere. He tossed it in her direction and Molly caught it.

'You have good reflexes.' Lots of things about her were good—better than good, with the notable exception of her decision to pursue and sleep with her best friend's husband.

Are you mad because she chose to sleep with Tariq or because she didn't sleep with you?

Molly raised herself back up, tilted her head in acknowledgement of his comment, and shook the water bottle. 'See, I did drink.'

'It is over half full. A person who doesn't take the desert seriously is asking for trouble,' he said, listening to the voice in his head echo his last few words. A man who was thinking about doing what he was thinking of doing was asking for more than simple trouble.

'I didn't ask to be in the desert. I didn't have a choice, and I would have thought it would have suited your sadistic tendencies if I had suffered heatstroke.' She levelled a glare filled with resentment at his face and then let herself fall back down on the bed. She winced as the action sent an extra-strong stab of pain through her temples.

With a curse Tair was on his knees at her side in seconds. 'Are you all right?'

'Don't fuss!' she said crankily. 'You've said I'm just overheated. I still am,' she murmured, tugging at the light cover fretfully. She had folded it down as far as her waist before she realised that she was only wearing her bra and pants. With a yelp she pulled the sheets up to her chin again and turned to him, eyes dark with suspicion.

'Where are my clothes?'

He nodded without much interest to the neat pile on the chair behind him. 'As I said, you were hot and you needed cooling down.' At that moment Tair's own internal thermostat could do with some adjustment. Her skin was alabaster and she had looked smooth and soft all over.

'Who undressed me?' The idea of Tair removing her clothes, and his hands touching her skin, sent a ripple of horror through her body—at least she hoped it was horror!

'It would bother you if it was me?'

Oh, God, he had!

Move on, she told herself, don't give it another thought—he probably hasn't. She recognised this as excellent advice but found it impossible to follow. She wasn't even wearing matching bra and pants, she realised.

As if that would have made any difference to him!

'I'm sure you would have enjoyed it more if it had been Beatrice.' She closed her eyes, waved goodbye to what little pride she'd had left, and willed the floor to open up at her feet.

The floor didn't open but her eyes did at his response.

'You want me to give you a mark from one to ten, Beatrice being the perfect ten!'

'I do not!'

He raised a dark brow. 'It sounded that way to me.'

Molly compressed her lips. 'I'm well aware that Beatrice is beautiful and I'm not. I happen to have two sisters who are just as gorgeous as Bea and I do not compete. I realise you have women falling over themselves for your attention but I don't beg for approval from men I don't even like.'

As Tair studied her angry flushed face he doubted she had any idea of how revealing her comment had been, but it did explain the awful clothes. Like many an ugly duckling, she had no idea she'd turned into a swan, and he felt irritated with the family that hadn't bothered telling her.

What did it take to make her realise?

'For the record, enjoyment is not something I feel when I see a woman unconscious and know I am responsible for her being that way.'

The hard note of self-recrimination in his soft voice made Molly stare as he dragged a hand through his dark hair.

'Beatrice is a beautiful woman. I know this even though I have never seen her in her underclothes.'

Molly's eyes fell. She had noted he hadn't said he wouldn't like to, but then realistically what man wouldn't? If Beatrice weren't so nice it would have been fun to hate her.

'But you are also a beautiful woman and I've never seen you in your underclothes.' His lean features suddenly melted into a grin. 'Barring that very brief but promising flash a moment ago.'

'You're disgusting!' she choked. He thinks I'm beautiful…? 'So you didn't…'

'No, that was Sabra—she was the only one brave enough.'

'Brave?'

'You scared them. You scared me…'

She narrowed her eyes for a moment—she had been almost taking him seriously.

'You stood there and screamed abuse at me, and manners are very highly rated among my mother's people.'

She shot into a sitting position, carrying the sheet with her. 'I have manners!' She looked at his mouth, felt her stomach muscles quiver and thought how she had far too many out-of-control hormones as well.

Tair watched as she swung her legs over the side of the divan. Her actions had the uncoordinated grace of a newly born foal. He felt a wave of totally unfamiliar tenderness as he struggled not to go to her aid. 'Just sit there and calm down. Next time I might not be quick enough to catch you.'

'I'm not going to faint…you caught me?'

His hooded glance connected with her wide eyes. 'Just.'

Wasn't that typical? The one time she got to be held in the arms of an incredible man she was unconscious—not, she tried to tell herself, that as a modern and liberated woman she craved being swept off her feet in any sense of the word!

She looked at him thorough her lashes, feeling unaccountably shy. 'I suppose I should say thank you for your quick reflexes…and I would if it hadn't been your fault that I fainted.'

His grin softened the severity of his stern expression and deepened the creases around his eyes. 'For a moment there I thought you were going soft on me.'

She tried to smile but her lips felt stiff, so instead she lifted her chin. 'There are times when even you seem almost human.'

His eyes contacted briefly with her own and for no reason at all Molly's heart started beating very fast.

Principles, he reminded himself, were not elastic just because his libido had gone into overdrive. 'There are times when I almost forget you slept with my married cousin last night.'

As a mood breaker his comment was highly effective.

The soft look in her eyes turned to cold dignity as she drew herself up ramrod-straight. 'As you mention it so often I find that hard to believe, but as you have such a bad memory perhaps I should write on here…bad woman…' She wiped a finger across her forehead, then glanced with distaste at the grime covering it. 'I need to wash.'

'I'll send someone in to help you.'

He turned and strode away in a flurry of long robes as though he couldn't get out fast enough.

'Probably afraid you'll contaminate him,' she told her reflection as she got to her feet. She ought to feel glad he had gone. The atmosphere had been getting a bit too…charged.

Intellectually she found him repellent, but the only problem was that it wasn't her intellect that was stimulated when she looked into his mesmerising eyes, or when he smiled, or even when he didn't smile. The fact was, she admitted with a sigh, the man was six feet four of rampant masculinity that would make any woman who wasn't dead from the waist down forget if she was actually not very highly sexed.

He was not a man she wanted to get involved with and, actually, the longer he carried on thinking she was poison, the better, because if he acted on the sexual attraction she sometimes felt was between them she wasn't sure if she was going to be able to respond on an intellectual level.

She was still exploring the room and trying to distract herself from thoughts of Tair and the strange fascination he exerted for her when a young girl, Sabra, appeared carrying food.

Molly, who was starving, sat on a pile of cushions at the low table the girl placed the tray on. The food, a spiced lamb dish with couscous and almonds, was melt-in-the-mouth delicious. When Molly told Sabra this in her not terribly good French, after she recognised that the girl didn't understand English, Sabra beamed with delight and immediately launched into a rapid speech in the same language.

Molly begged with the help of hand gestures for Sabra to slow down, but eventually understood that when she had finished eating she could bathe if she wished to.

Miming disgust when she touched her face, Molly assured Sabra that she definitely wished to!

CHAPTER EIGHT

'WHERE would you run to?'

Her hand on the heavy curtain at the door of the tent, Molly spun around, with her hair, still damp from her bath, swinging around her startled face.

Tair's head was bare and his dark hair, gleaming blue-black in the candlelight, was tousled and damp, as if he too had just bathed. The flowing robes he had worn earlier were gone to reveal a white tee shirt that clung disturbingly close to his hard-muscled torso, and moleskin riding breeches tucked into leather riding boots.

She let go of the curtain and it fell back into place with a swishing sound that seemed awfully final.

'I'm not running but, as you ask, any place would be better than here. I was actually looking for Sabra.'

'If you knew the desert you would not say that, *ma belle*,' he said drily.

'I'm not your "*belle*," or anything else of yours.'

He revealed his teeth in a wolfish smile and looked amused by her acid tone. 'There is no place to run, Molly. Accept it.'

His seductive voice was like rich, warm honey.

Molly struggled to maintain her attitude of angry defiance

while she fought not to recognise the part of her that didn't want to run.

'Why—because you say so?' She gave a contemptuous snort and felt her heart beating like a trapped bird in her chest as he took a step towards her.

His appearance was the essence of primitive, raw masculinity. Looking at him made her ache with longing.

'What did you want to ask Sabra? She has looked after you?'

'Yes, the food was marvellous.'

'The bathing facilities met with your approval?'

She nodded, the bathing facilities having been positively decadent. She had been reluctant to leave the deep scented water and her skin still glowed with the sweet-smelling oils that Sabra had shyly supplied for her use.

'I was going to ask Sabra about the sleeping arrangements. I'm assuming that I'm allowed some privacy.'

He had stopped a few feet away from her, close enough for her to be able to trace that thin white scar with her eyes. She wondered what it would feel like to trace it with her tongue, and then wished she hadn't as her face grew hot.

'The sleeping arrangements are entirely your choice.' His eyes slid from her face to the low divan piled with silken cushions. 'But it can get lonely at night.'

Molly swallowed and folded her arms across her chest in an instinctively protective gesture. 'I'm quite comfortable with my own company, thank you.'

'Don't worry—you won't have to protect your virtue. I have never felt the need to force a woman.'

The contempt in his voice stung. 'Just so long as you know I could and would.'

'My taste doesn't run to beige creatures.' Although anything less beige than the woman glaring at him with luminous eyes would, he admitted, have been difficult to imagine. His critical gaze ran over her crumpled skirt and blouse before he gave a faint grimace. 'Why are you wearing those things? I asked Sabra to give you some fresh clothes.'

Molly knew there were some women who got told by beautiful men they were gorgeous and she knew that she was not one of them. All the same his dismissive contempt stung.

'She did, but I prefer to wear my own clothes. And while we're on the subject of taste, mine doesn't run to...' Molly struggled to speak past the sudden constriction in her aching throat as she stared straight at his chest '...to men who kidnap me.'

'Think of it as a little adventure.'

Molly, who was thinking that the way her skin prickled with heat when she looked at him was insanity, gave a faint scornful snort... She was having a big problem with words.

'Try and be philosophical about this. Concentrate on the plus points.'

'Because there are so many?'

He laughed and Molly tried hard to maintain her attitude of defiance as her eyes clashed with his bold, glittering stare.

'When else would you have had the opportunity to study at such close...intimate quarters a foreign culture?' His voice had the seductive texture of warm silk. The sort of silk that would feel sensuous against your skin.

'If I want to know about foreign culture I'll read a book in the comfort of my armchair.'

It was one thing to be caught in a trap, it was another thing entirely to turn the key in the lock yourself, then give it to your jailer.

That would be crazy, and only crazy people would give into a sudden attraction that blazed for a short time, then left cold ashes of regret behind.

It wasn't a question of whether Tair would respect her in the morning if they spent the night together—he didn't respect her now—but it was a question of whether she would respect herself.

'There are some things you can't learn from a book.'

Their eyes connected and the blaze in his blitzed every sane thought from her head. As the stare lengthened the static hum in the air became a loud buzz in her ears. Every instinct of self-preservation she had screamed at her not to ask him what those things were—in her present state of mind and body she might like what she heard!

Get a grip, she advised herself as she lowered her gaze. Her skin felt so acutely sensitive that she was conscious of the feathery prickle of her lashes against her hot cheek as she struggled to control her uneven breaths.

'You're not one of those people who travel to foreign places and stay safely cocooned in sterile luxury behind the high resort walls?'

'In case it has slipped your memory, I'm not on holiday.'

Tair, who didn't deign to acknowledge her dry interjection, expanded on his theme, his low voice pitched barely above a sinfully seductive whisper that was doing all manner of damage to her nervous system.

'I think a person should seize the chance of new experiences whenever possible. If you don't,' he mused, 'who knows? You might live to regret it…?'

And he would, he knew, always regret it if he did not follow the instincts that a midnight ride through a starlit desert landscape had been unable to diminish.

He had been appalled to find himself actually looking for excuses for her behaviour…and reminding himself that she was all the things he despised in a woman and it had not lessened the fire that burned in his blood.

Their glances met but after a moment she lowered her eyes in apparent confusion.

'I do not expect the *ingénue* act. You do not need to play
the part with me.'

Molly, wishing it weren't an act, forced herself to look at
him. 'So all in all this is just a tremendous opportunity to
expand my horizons?'

'A situation is what you make of it.'

'Silly me. I hadn't realised how lucky I am to be abducted
against my will by a man who is a throwback to the good old
days when a man was a man and a woman was a slave!'

'I don't require a slave.'

She stuck out her chin, stubbornly refusing to acknowledge
the message in his gleaming eyes.

'I wasn't applying.' With a pretended cool she looked dis-
missively up the long, lean, muscle-packed length of vital
body. Feeling her cool slip, she lowered her glance and gave
a cynical snort. 'I don't suppose you need anything or anyone.'
Tair took self-reliance to a new level.

'I wouldn't say that.'

A note she had not heard in his voice before brought her
head up. Tired of skirting around the issue, she said what she
had been thinking. 'Are you trying to seduce me?'

'Yes.'

The single raw word did more damage to her resolve than
all the candlelit dinners and romantic gestures in the world—
not that Tair would have offered her either.

The breath left her lungs in one long sibilant sigh as a
pulse of longing slammed through Molly's body. Her eyes half
closed, her breath coming fast, she leaned towards him, her
body drawn as though by an invisible force. Every individual
cell vibrated with the force of the desire that crashed over her
like waves pounding on the shore as she lifted her face to his.

Tair stepped forward and lifted his hand to tangle his
fingers into the sleek mesh of her hair and smooth back the

silky strands that clung to her cheeks before framing her face between his big hands.

He was torn. He wanted to touch her with a need that threatened to consume him, but when he did he was conscious of a vulnerability inside him, an emptiness that he didn't want to acknowledge was there.

But he had to touch her.

As his thumbs moved over the curve of her cheeks he could feel her tremble with passion.

'What are you doing to me? Every time I look at your face, think of your mouth or the curve of your neck…' Unable to resist the desire to taste her any longer, he pressed his mouth to her throat.

Molly gave a fractured sigh as her head fell back. He ran his fingers slowly down the exposed column of pale skin, then, giving in to the silent invitation, he kissed his way slowly back up.

By the time he reached her mouth Molly couldn't breathe.

'Your skin tastes like flowers.'

Molly's heavy lids lifted as he tilted her face up to his. She stared greedily at him, memorising each primitive angle, every chiselled plane, and thought how she wished he would kiss her again soon because she was dying already.

It wasn't until he said, 'I couldn't have that on my conscience,' that she realised she had said it, not thought it.

'This is happening?'

'If you doubt it I'm doing something wrong.'

'I don't think that's possible.'

He laughed, but the laughter didn't last and there were lines of strain etched in his face that Molly didn't see because the raw hunger in his eyes blinded her.

The warm well of excitement in her belly flared hot as he slowly angled her face first one way and then the other.

'You're beautiful.'

For once in her life Molly felt it, and anticipation made the pulses deep in her body throb as his face came close to hers. Tair whispered her name, his deep voice making her nerve endings tingle as he added throatily, 'So you want to be seduced?'

'I want you.'

'And I want you.'

'I thought I was beige…?' She groaned as his lips once again found her neck. Clinging to a thin strand of remaining sanity, she gasped. 'Oh, I really don't think this is a good idea.'

He nipped at the soft fullness of her lower lip and then traced the trembling outline of her mouth with the tip of his tongue. Her heavy lids lifted as he nudged the side of her nose with his, and his dark face swam into vision as she felt as much as heard his husky whisper.

'Sometimes bad is more fun than good.'

Holding her gaze with his hot blue eyes, he fitted his mouth to hers and kissed her slowly at first, then deeper, parting her lips and sliding his tongue into the warm moistness of her mouth.

'You taste so good,' he said against her mouth.

She slid her fingers into his thick lush hair and said, 'So do you,' in a fierce little voice before kissing him back hard.

She felt the vibration of a warm laugh in his chest, but soon he was kissing her some more with a hungry, bruising intensity and the force of her response made her tremble.

When his head lifted Tair was breathing hard, dragging air into his lungs through flared nostrils. She saw the tension in him now, felt it as he stood there like a man who was fighting against invisible bonds.

'If you look at me like that I'll…' His eyes darkened as he scanned her upturned features with a fierce predatory expression that made her insides dissolve like sugar in hot liquid. 'Have you any idea what your mouth has been doing to me?' he groaned.

She shook her head and lifted a hand to his cheek. Her lips parted, her expression rapt as she trailed a finger down the stubble-roughened curve of his cheek before tracing the line of the small white scar.

'How did you do that?' she whispered.

He said something indistinct, but even if he had shouted Molly wouldn't have been able to hear it; all she could hear was the throb of blood pulsing through her veins.

When he turned his head and touched his open mouth to the centre of her palm a fractured gasp escaped her aching throat. And when he took hold of her wrist and trailed kisses along the blue-veined inner aspect of her forearm the strength drained from her limbs.

An earthy moan of shocked pleasure left her lips as she felt his erection dig into the softness of her belly. 'You're…'

Tair smiled a fierce smile that made her skin prickle with dark heat. Her eyes squeezed closed as he bent his head, his fingers skimming under the neck of her blouse as he kissed her, increasing the erotic pressure.

Molly felt as though she were drowning in a swirling sea of sensation. She was painfully conscious of her body in a way that she never had been before, conscious of how her soft curves fitted into his hard angles.

She could smell the scent of soap on his skin mingled with the warm musky scent of his body and it sent a stab of lust through her. She leaned into him, holding on tight to his narrow waist because her legs would no longer support her. She could feel the taut muscles and the edge of his ribcage, and as their eyes met his were so hot and hungry that she felt dizzy with sheer wanting just looking at him.

'You are the most beautiful man, Tair, so beautiful. I can't stand up.'

'That works for me,' he growled, scooping her up into his

arms and striding towards the low divan. He laid her down with a tenderness that was in stark contrast to the fierce need in his face.

'I still don't like you.'

He arranged his long lean length beside her and pushed the silky skein of hair back from her face.

'Do you suppose we could discuss this later?'

She nodded. 'I just thought I should be honest.'

'Your honesty is appreciated.'

'I do want you though.' She couldn't stop staring at his fingers as they slipped the buttons of her shirt undone. He had to be feeling her heart, it was thumping so hard against her ribcage.

'That was the message I was getting.'

She ran the tip of her tongue across her dry lips. 'You're trembling.' She could feel the shudders that were running through his taut frame.

'So are you.'

'There is something I have to say.'

'Not now.'

'About me and Tariq—he *really* is—'

'Definitely not now!' A nerve clenching in his cheek, he laid a finger against her lips and levered himself upright.

It took several deep breaths before the image in his head was extinguished and he could control the swell of mindless jealousy.

For a moment she thought he was going to walk away. The relief when he didn't was intense. Lying there, she watched as he pushed a few cushions out of the way and propped his broad shoulders against the carved headboard.

'Just shut up, come here and let me undress you, *ma belle*. I have been thinking about unwrapping you all day.'

CHAPTER NINE

MOLLY looked at the hand Tair stretched out towards her. She might not know much, but she knew a no-going-back moment when she saw one and this was it.

For a second she just stared at his hand, so much darker compared to her own, the fingers long and sensitive, a strong hand.

Her eyes lifted, and she thought how he was a strong man. A man with passion and conviction. One conviction unfortunately being that she was a home-wrecking tart, so it seemed safe to assume that his feelings for her had very little to do with respect.

This should have mattered, but by this point it didn't. She expelled the breath that had been trapped in her lungs in one shuddering sigh and stretched out her own hand to him.

Tair's fingers closed around hers, their eyes met in a moment of mutual understanding and then he pulled her towards him.

'That's right,' he approved as she put her knees either side of his thighs.

Her face was level with his when Molly, still kneeling with her skirt hitched above her knees, laid her hands either side of his face then in the same seamless action kissed him firmly on the mouth.

For a split second he didn't respond, but when he did it was as if a touch-paper had been ignited and the flame was contagious. When she met his tongue with her own and the kiss deepened her hips unconsciously moved with the same sensuous motion as her mouth.

Tair breathed words against her mouth in his own language, words she understood on a primal level. Words that made her skin crackle with heat and her quivering stomach muscles grow heavy with desire.

When Tair laid his hands on her shoulders Molly responded to the pressure, her skirt riding farther up, and she sat down, gasping sharply as the sensitive apex of her legs made contact with his hard thighs.

The raw desire in his face shook her to the core and made the excitement pulsing inside her expand. Her heart swelled with emotion… She wanted to give herself to him more than she wanted to take her next breath.

His cerulean eyes didn't leave hers for a second as he undid the last few buttons of her shirt and peeled it off her shoulders. A moment later the blouse was flung away.

A heartbeat later her bra followed.

She lifted her hands in an instinctive gesture, but with a growl he caught her wrists and held them firmly to her sides.

'I want to look at you. Don't hide yourself, Molly… never hide yourself from me.'

His eyes fell and she held her breath. It seemed impossible that someone who embodied every male physical attribute there was could be impressed by her unfeminine angles.

But amazingly he was.

'Dear, sweet…' His powerful chest lifted as a deep shuddering sigh moved through his body.

Molly felt the helpless response of her own sensitised flesh respond to his scrutiny. The tingling life that pulled the pink buds of her small trembling breasts to tight prominence was painful, but not in a bad way.

'You're so beautiful, so perfect…'

Tair drank in the sight of her, the delicate bones of her shoulders, the shape of her narrow ribcage and the soft twin mounds of her high, deliciously plump breasts. To watch them visibly respond to the feel of his eyes made him think about how sensitive they would be to his touch.

He closed a hand over one small firm mound of trembling flesh and then the next, his thumb moving across each tight nub, drawing a series of small throaty gasps from her parted lips.

'Like sweet, ripe little apples.'

His bent his head and ran his tongue across the tip of one quivering peak. Her back arched as she grabbed the back of his head to hold him there.

'Oh, God, Tair, you…'

With her eyes closed, her splayed fingers sank deep into the lush pelt of his hair, then tightened as his tongue began to explore and tease, evoking sensations inside her that she had not dreamt existed.

It was just about the most erotic image she had ever imagined, but the feelings it produced went farther. Right now, though, Molly would make no attempt to unravel the complex tangle of emotions that erupted when she looked at his mouth against her body.

When Tair lifted his head he was breathing hard and there were lines of dark colour etched along the contours of his high cheekbones.

Without a word Molly reached out and began to unfasten the buttons on his shirt.

He sat still, looking at the top of her bent head, fighting against the fire in his veins and the urge to rip apart the buttons of his shirt as her trembling fingers performed the task with what felt to him like agonising slowness.

His control lasted until she reached the last two buttons and then he could bear it no longer. With a groan he tore the shirt open sending the buttons flying across the room.

Molly sucked in a deep breath, her eyes darkening and her pupils expanding as she watched his muscles ripple beneath skin that gleamed like oiled satin.

Things tightened and stirred deep inside her and the heavy ache low down in her body intensified as her greedy gaze slid down his bronzed torso.

He had the perfect body. His shoulders were broad, his chest was covered in a light dusting of dark hair and his stomach was washboard-flat. There wasn't an ounce of surplus flesh on his body to blur the perfect muscle definition on display.

The stab of lustful heat that slid through her body made her gasp.

Tair swallowed, the muscles in his brown throat visibly contracting as he reached for the buckle on his belt and slid it from his narrow hips. 'Come, I need to feel your skin against mine.'

Molly, her eyes locked on his, placed a hand on the headboard either side of his head as she leaned forward. Tair placed one hand in the small of her back and the other behind her head. As their lips met in a deep, drowning kiss he jerked her up hard against him.

Molly's breasts were crushed against his chest and she moaned into his mouth as Tair's fingers tangled in her hair, and opened her mouth to deepen the kiss. She felt Tair's hands moving over her back, drawing her even closer to him.

But not close enough! Never close enough…to satisfy the knot of frustration inside her that tightened another painful notch. 'I want…'

When he pulled away the febrile glow in his eyes made her head spin. 'What do you want?'

'Everything. All of you.'

Without a word he slid down the bed and flipped her over onto her back. Molly's heart skipped as she saw the look in his eyes, the heat, and his hunger. She could feel them in her bones.

A moment later he pulled her beneath him and carried on kissing her with a frantic need that bruised her lips. She kissed him back, wanting it never to stop, loving the weight of his body on hers, loving the roughness of his jaw on her soft skin, loving the smell and taste of him.

There was nothing about him that didn't feel perfect and right.

She hadn't expected that feeling... The thought flitted through her brain and then his fingers were sliding under the waistband of her skirt, easing it down over her hips, and she couldn't think anything beyond please...and yes!

Tair levered himself off her, his intention to remove his boots and trousers distracted by the sight of her lying there so wanton and so willing, her tight nipples still wet from his ministrations.

'You are totally and absolutely...' He bent forward and kissed her stomach, letting his hands slide slowly down her slim hips. He marvelled at the texture of her skin and how the lightest touch made her tremble and shake.

She moaned his name, her back arching as his mouth slid lower leaving a wet trail on the soft curve of her belly. With a cry he forced himself from her.

'Remember where we were. I need to...' He pulled off one boot and flashed her a look that made things inside her twist.

Even with his back to her Tair was aware of her big eyes watching his every move as he pulled off his second boot and then kicked aside his trousers and shorts. The knowledge that she was watching him increased the painful level of his arousal.

The line of his back and narrow hips, the length of his leg, the tautness of his male buttocks looked to Molly like a classical statue come to life. Then he turned and as her eyes slid down his body she forgot about statues and his classical grace.

The heat flooded her face as she struggled to lift her gaze, or, failing that, even blink or breathe.

Sucking in air through her nostrils, she shook her head and closed her eyes as all her lust and hunger fused into one intense ache of primitive yearning to have him inside her.

A deep, almost animal groan was ripped from his throat as he threw himself down beside her, rolling her onto her side until they lay face to face. Then he placed a hand in the small of her back and pulled her thigh across his hip.

'Have you noticed we fit really well?'

Molly, who on recent evidence was having doubts on this score, didn't say anything—she wasn't sure she could speak without crying... Was lust meant to feel this emotional? In all other ways it had outstripped her most optimistic expectations.

Tair nuzzled her throat before parting her lips with his tongue. Still kissing her, he took her hand and fed it onto his body, curling her fingers around his shaft.

He sucked in a deep breath as her fingers tightened and when he slid his own hand between her legs she gasped. Then a moment later she sighed and pressed against his hand.

'This is for me?' he asked, sliding his fingers over her wetness and drawing sighs and cries from her as she rolled on her back and parted her thighs for him in silent invitation.

He kissed her and nuzzled her neck and watched as her back arched. A gasp deeper than any that had preceded it was wrenched from her parted lips as he slid a finger inside her.

Molly could feel his heartbeat as he lowered himself onto her, his hands either side of her face. She grabbed his shoulders, her fingers spread across his sweat-slick skin.

The nudge of the hot, silky-skinned tip of his erection against the apex of her parted thighs made Molly stiffen. Then Tair kissed and breathed words into her ear and she relaxed, though she was unable to stop tensing as he entered her.

'I can't!'

Above her Tair had gone very still.

'There is no *I* just *we…we* can, we will…just let it happen, *ma belle*, let me make it happen for you. Look at me, go with me…'

Molly responded to the coaxing of the velvet voice and opened her eyes as he slid another inch inside her.

'Oh, God, Tair, this is…'

'It will be,' he promised thickly. 'It will be…'

The breath left her lungs in a long sibilant sigh as he began to move.

Tair held her hips, murmuring her name thickly as he slid slowly deeper and deeper into her sweet slickness, then he repeated the process again and again, all the time conscious of the pressure he fought to control inside him building and burning.

As he felt Molly tighten around his length Tair's mind slipped into a dark primal gear where there was nothing in his world but the woman who cried his name as she moved beneath him and the need—the necessity—to reach a plateau where they could merge and be one.

Molly's entire being was focused on the incredible sensations she was experiencing, of Tair inside her, stretching and filling her. She felt things tighten in anticipation as the pleasure centres of her brain overloaded.

Tair watched her face, saw the rosy flush wash over her skin and her eyes widen in shock as the first soft flutters of climax hit her. Then he felt the vibration of the feral groan that came from deep inside her as her muscles began to spasm.

Tair let himself go, then allowed himself the final deep

thrust into her as he was engulfed by a mind-shattering and spirit-lifting release.

For several minutes he lay on top of her until his heartbeat slowly returned to within shouting distance of normality.

When he rolled away she cuddled up to his side like a kitten and laid her head on his chest. It was one thing to take a conniving woman of experience to his bed, but it was, as they said, a whole different ball game to take a virgin!

'You didn't sleep with Tariq.' A bemused frown creased Tair's brow as he absently trailed his fingers down the curve of her spine. Molly arched her back under the pressure and almost purred.

'Don't be stupid!'

'He went into your bedroom. I saw him.'

His jaw clenched as he recalled how he had seen with his own eyes that Tariq was unable to take his eyes off her. The only way a man who wanted Molly could remain pure was if he removed himself to another continent!

'Men and women can do other things besides have sex in a bedroom.' Although not in Tair's bedroom, she thought.

'He was never your lover?' Tair's expression hardened to one of predatory possessiveness as he looked down at her silky head and thought how Tariq would now never be.

He would do everything within his power to make sure that Tariq never got near Molly again in his life.

'You've never slept with any man.' The wheels in Tair's mind seemed to be working tortuously slowly.

'No, I told you—Tariq and Khalid, they're my half-brothers.'

'Be seri—' She felt him stiffen. 'My God, he is…they are…Susan Al Kamal, the woman who divorced…she remarried?'

Molly nodded.

'You're Susan Al Kamal's daughter?'

Molly turned her face into his warm skin, breathing in the warm musky smell of him. 'And a bit of an embarrassment to the Al Kamals, the skeleton in the closet.'

He cursed softly in his own tongue and groaned.

'I did try and tell you.'

She heard him curse once more before he said, 'What have I done?'

'I thought you were the expert…' Her teasing tone faded as she added, 'Does it matter who my mother was?'

He caught her chin in his hand and brought her face up to his. 'Matter…you ask does it matter? I have taken your innocence.'

She watched, her sense of bewilderment increasing as he groaned and rolled onto his back. As he lay there with his eyes closed the tendons in his neck were tense as he dragged in air through his flared nostrils.

'I wasn't *innocent*, just *inexperienced*,' she said, allowing her eyes to roam over the sleek strong lines of his tautly muscled body before she turned on her side.

A hissing noise of exasperation escaped his lips as he opened his eyes and fixed her with a bright blue incredulous stare.

'You were a virgin.'

'You did nothing I didn't want you to, even if I didn't know that's what I wanted at the time.' He had intuitively known exactly how to please her, how to send her to heaven.

'Look at me.'

'I am.' It was possible she might never be able to stop!

'You must realise that this changes everything… Tariq is your half-brother, you were living under the protection of the royal house and I abducted you.'

'It doesn't have to change anything. I'll tell Tariq I came because I wanted to just the way you put it on the letter.'

Tair loosed an odd laugh. 'You think that would matter? You are not just *any* woman. If you were any woman I would take you as my mistress.' Until thirty seconds ago that had been his intention. 'But that of course is now out of the question.'

'Would I have had any say in the matter?' He acted as if she would have left her life at a word from him…a word he'd just made plain wasn't going to come her way now.

Tair, his face set into grim lines, did not even respond to her ironic comment. 'We must marry, of course.'

She searched his face, saw that he looked pale and his expression was darkly sombre. 'You're not serious…?'

'I have never been more serious.'

Molly shook her head, gathered the silk sheet around herself and swung her legs over the side of the bed. She was shaking. She had to break it to this man who was clearly living in a bygone century when family honour and a woman's reputation required preserving at all costs that things no longer worked this way. She tried to speak calmly.

'Don't be stupid. I can't marry you… You don't know me or love me or—'

His voice, terse and impatient, cut across her. 'This is not a question of love.'

Always a good thing to say when proposing.

She slung an incredulous look over her shoulder. He was lying there, one arm curved above his head, looking more incredible than any man had a right to look.

'It is,' he told her plainly, 'a question of honour.'

'Your honour, not mine. I'm living in the twenty-first century.'

Tariq shook his head and conceded, 'I know it's not something either of us planned to happen, but you'll get used to the idea.'

'Have you been listening to a word I've said?'

'Some women would not be insulted by the proposal.'

'I'm not some women.' The heat flared in her cheeks.

'My wife…'

She stuck out her chin. 'Don't be ludicrous.'

Her childish refusal to recognise the gravity of the situation frustrated him. 'Grow up, Molly. This is not what either of us would want, but in life there are consequences for our actions. You think *I* wanted this to happen?' he yelled, revealing suddenly that he wasn't as composed about this as he appeared.

'Thanks! Strange, but you didn't seem to be a man who was doing something against his will a few minutes ago!'

He looked irritated. 'That isn't what I meant! It has always been expected that I will marry to further the political and financial interest of our country…'

'A family tradition—how sweet,' she trilled. 'I wouldn't like to stand in the way of such romance,' she choked.

His lips tightened. 'That is obviously no longer possible.' His glance slid over her slim, stiff figure and a gleam ignited deep in his eyes. 'Still, there are plus points…' His hand suddenly shot out and curled around her arm.

'You know what I think?' She gave a grunt of anger as he pulled her back down onto the bed beside him.

'What do you think, Molly James?'

Tair watched her brush a gleaming strand of hair from her face as she glared up at him, breathing hard. He felt his recently satiated lust stir as he looked down into her angry golden eyes.

'I think that you slept with me because you thought you could make me forget any other man I'd ever been with…including, you thought, Tariq. Abducting me wasn't enough— you had to be doubly sure.'

Actually what she said made a lot of sense, supposing he was as cold and calculating as she apparently thought. The irony was that where Molly James was concerned he was incapable of thinking beyond touching her—clinical objectivity did not even register on his radar!

'You think I'm that good?'

The colour flew to her cheeks at the throaty taunt. 'Don't give me that,' she snapped. 'You know you are!' A woman who slept with Tair would forever be comparing future lovers with him and finding them sadly wanting.

The mocking light left his deepset sapphire eyes as he studied her face. 'It takes two…sometimes two people just mesh.' He took her chin gently in his hand and shook his head. 'It is rare, Molly.'

'Don't turn this into something it isn't. We had sex…I'm not marrying you because of some warped idea you have of honour and stuff. Tariq won't feel that way. He's modern… he's not a barbarian.'

'You think I am barbarian? You are reluctant to marry me because I don't have nice manners?'

A beautiful barbarian. 'I think this would have been a one-night stand if you hadn't cottoned on to the fact I was telling the truth when I said Tariq was my half-brother.'

'Is that what this is about? You think all I want is a one-night stand? You really think I'm going to leave in the morning? You think that in two days' time I was going to wave goodbye to you for ever?'

She swallowed. 'Weren't.you?'

He shook his head and the blaze in his eyes held her as surely as his arms. 'I'm not going anywhere,' he promised, stroking the side of her face with his finger. 'Do you think that one night would be enough for me? I can't get enough of you, *ma belle*. Be honest, Molly—you don't want me to leave you now, do you?'

Molly told herself he was only saying these things because he wanted to make her agree to marrying him. 'I'm not marrying you.'

She sighed and turned her face into his palm. Just at the

edge of her consciousness there lurked the knowledge that there was a limit to how honest she could allow herself to be!

But there was one thing she couldn't deny!

'I don't think I can get enough of you, Tair,' she admitted quietly.

She watched satisfaction, male and primitive, flare in his eyes and it was mingled with a tenderness that almost stopped her heart.

He bent towards her and her soft lips parted under the pressure of his mouth. Molly curled her arms around his neck as he kissed her deeply. His warm breath fanned over her cheek as their noses nudged and he speared his long fingers into her hair.

'I think you might have changed your mind about not being able to have enough of me by the morning, *ma belle*.'

'I might surprise you.'

'Now that is a claim I would like to put to the test.'

'This doesn't mean I'll marry you.'

His husky laugh was lost in her mouth.

CHAPTER TEN

'SO YOU'RE awake. I am disappointed. I was looking forward to waking you up.'

They had made love long into the night but when Molly had fallen asleep it had been deeply. She had not stirred when Tair had left their bed.

She didn't turn her head when he spoke, but held on tighter to the silk sheet she had wrapped sarong-wise about herself and allowed the hair she had anchored away from her face with her forearm to fall free to screen her face like a silken curtain.

'If you were looking forward to it so very much maybe you shouldn't have sneaked away while I was asleep.'

'I was not quiet, I made a great deal of noise, and if it makes you feel any better I had no desire to leave you, but there were certain matters that needed attending to.'

'I don't need to feel better. I feel totally fine.'

'What are you doing?'

She flashed him a scornful look but felt her stomach muscles quiver as she did— God, he looked incredible. She quickly diverted her eyes. 'What does it look like? What have you done with my clothes?'

'Relax. They will be returned to you when they are laundered.'

Molly straightened up. Was he kidding? How could she relax now? 'And what am I meant to do in the meantime?' she enquired. 'Or is this the way you like your women?' she asked, her eyes looking down to her own bare toes. 'Barefoot and tied to the kitchen sink?'

'This is not a kitchen.'

'Kitchen, bed—what's the difference? You know exactly what I mean.' She stopped and drew breath, thinking if he did know it was more than she did! She seemed to know nothing any more. Meeting him had turned her entire life upside down. 'And I,' she added hastily, 'am not a woman…that is, I am…a woman, obviously.'

It was certainly obvious that she was from where Tair was standing. He felt his desire stir as his glance dropped to the outline of her nipples pushing against the thin silk.

'Just not your woman…well, obviously…because, well, I'm my own woman…person…'

'You are very politically correct this morning, though not very accurate.'

Better late than never, Molly thought.

'You are my woman and you will be my wife.'

She ignored the little thrill of excitement inside her. 'My God, but you really are a male chauvinist! I thought you'd forgotten that daft idea by now.'

'But *your* male chauvinist, Molly Mouse.'

'How do you know I want you?'

'Because you were very convincing last night when you told me you did.' His husky laughter only intensified her blush. 'There are clothes there.'

'I can't wear any of those.'

She glanced to a pile of garments neatly stacked and gave a regretful sigh. The rich colours and sumptuous fabrics were beautiful, but not for her. 'Don't you have anything…?'

'In beige?' Tair suggested. He revealed his even white teeth in a sardonic grin and shook his head. 'Definitely not.'

'There is nothing wrong with beige,' she retorted with dignity. 'Some of my favourite outfits are beige.'

'Of that I have no doubt,' he said drily. 'But alas we have no beige or taupe or even mushroom. So it is this or nothing.'

'Were you born delivering ultimatums?'

Tair watched her eyes flash with militant fire. Aggressiveness was not a quality he admired in a woman, which made the stirrings of tenderness he felt when he watched her little chin lift all the more inexplicable. It could be that there were worse things in life than being married to Molly James.

'Were you born being pointlessly stubborn?' he retorted.

'I was born a clean slate, but I was brought up not to take orders from egotistical men.'

He gave an irritated click of his tongue. 'I am not attempting to subjugate you, just dress you.'

It was undressing that he was better suited to.

A hazy heat filmed her amber eyes as the memories of last night flooded back. She could still hear his harsh intake of breath as he had exposed her breasts. It seemed as if, once awoken, her sensation-saturated nerve endings might never return to normal.

'I can dress myself,' she protested.

He lifted a filmy diaphanous shawl from the selection of items, and let it slip slowly through his fingers. He arched a brow. 'Wear this or nothing?'

Lips pursed, she stared defiantly. 'Then it's nothing.'

He gave one of his inimical shrugs. 'Fair enough.'

'Right, good, then…'

'I have no problem with your decision, though the more conservative-minded might be a little less open-minded about you walking around naked.'

'You know that's not what I meant,' she replied, infuriated with herself for blushing.

Tair's glance drifted over the smooth curve of her cheek and dropped to her mouth. 'A man is allowed his fantasies.' And he had never expected his to be fulfilled by a virgin who had a tongue that was as sharp as her skin was soft.

Molly knew that he was only being flippant, but the knowledge that she was part of his fantasies made her shiver in delight.

'The idea excites me.' The discovery brought a predatory gleam to his deep-set blue eyes.

'Well, it disgusts me!' she retorted. 'I would never walk around naked in front of any man!' That would require confidence or a killer body and she had neither.

'I would hope not. However, I think you will enjoy walking around naked in front of me.'

She opened her mouth, but the protest died on her tongue as she saw the blaze of hunger in his eyes.

'It's all about the chase with men.'

'I know you're not speaking from personal experience.'

'Because no man would chase me?'

A spasm of irritation crossed his lean face. 'Not in the beige outfit,' he agreed drily. His brow furrowed as he studied her face. 'I cannot understand why you constantly pull yourself down. You hide your beauty in the baggy clothes, you scrape back your beautiful hair, yet even in beige your innate sensuality still shines through.

'As for men and the chase—yes, there is some element of truth in that. We are programmed to chase, and sometimes the pursuit is more exciting than what is at the end of it, but with you…that is not so. You are the most exciting woman I have ever slept with and, in case you did not realise, the only virgin. Now I will leave you to dress.'

And he did just that, having reduced Molly to a state of open-mouthed shock.

* * *

The beaded hem of the silk gown swished sexily against her legs as she walked. The fabric had a sensual feel against her bare skin. She couldn't decide if it was her imagination, but she felt that the dress made her walk differently, with more of a sexy sway to her hips.

Maybe it was the silk that made her more conscious of her own femininity?

Molly was turning over the theory that the changes went deeper, that maybe it was less about the fabric brushing against her bare legs as she moved and more about her newly discovered sensuality, when she spotted the unmistakable tall, lean figure standing some distance away.

Molly immediately stopped theorising, she stopped thinking and even her breathing was a hit-and-miss affair. The ache of longing as she stared at him made her burn with emotions she was terrified to acknowledge.

He was beautiful.

'He's my lover.'

But not my husband.

Her hands clenched so hard that her nails left half-moon impressions in the soft flesh of her palms as she stared across at Tair.

He was talking to another man who was leading two horses that pawed the ground impatiently as Tair said something that made the other man laugh out loud.

Then suddenly, as if he sensed her eyes on him, Tair turned his head sharply. It was impossible from this distance for her to make out his expression and even if he had been closer his eyes were hidden behind a pair of designer shades.

He stood motionless and Molly's heart began to thud, the sound echoing in her ears as wave after wave of powerful, enervating lust and longing crashed over her.

There was activity in the compound, but Molly felt as if she were wrapped in a pocket of stillness. A stillness that was broken when one of the horses, spooked by a loud noise, began to dance restlessly. As the man Tair had been talking to struggled to calm the second horse, the spooked animal pulled free, rose up on his hind legs and began to paw the air.

Tair stepped forward, making no visible attempt to avoid the flailing hooves that were perilously close to his head.

Molly held her breath. Tair seemed to be speaking to the animal but it seemed to her that words were a pretty poor defence against razor-sharp hooves attached to several hundred pounds of equine muscle!

Why didn't he just walk away as any person with half a brain would?

'Oh, God!' she groaned, fear like an icy fist in her belly as the flashing hooves whistled past Tair's head and the snorting horse danced just out of reach.

For pity's sake, what was he trying to do to her?

Teeth clenched, breath coming in short, shallow gasps, she stood, her eyes glued to the scene. 'Stupid man!' she whispered.

Just because he looked like a god, did he think that quality extended to immortality?

An image of Tair lying pale and still on the floor, his lifeblood seeping from the serrated edges of a wound, superimposed itself over her vision. She shook her head to banish it. This was one of those moments when a vivid imagination was a definite curse!

Her heart was in her mouth as he advanced slowly, his hands held wide and all the time talking to the animal.

'You're going in the wrong direction, you crazy man.' Sensible people ran in the opposite direction when they encountered danger. He seemed to rush to meet it.

A silence fell over the encampment as Tair came close enough to pat the gleaming black flank of the wild-eyed animal. Molly couldn't believe what she was seeing when he laid his head close to the steaming horse's mane.

Molly's expression was now one of reluctant fascination. And she wasn't the only person held in thrall. People had stopped what they were doing to watch this masterly display. Tair, apparently oblivious to the hush, carried on speaking to the animal.

Molly shook her head. It was totally amazing when barely two minutes later the animal was nuzzling Tair's palm like a lamb. Tair responded with a laugh to some comment from the man holding the other horse and then glanced towards Molly.

A moment later he vaulted lightly onto the horse's bare back. The reins in one hand, he nudged the animal's flanks and the horse, responding to the pressure of the rider's thighs, broke into a canter.

Man and animal stopped a couple of feet from her. They made a pretty impressive picture, both beautiful and untamed.

Molly folded her arms across her chest and maintained an unimpressed expression that slipped when the horse pawed the ground. She stepped backwards nervously, pretending she hadn't seen Tair grin.

'He won't hurt you.'

No, but you will, she thought as he leaned down to pat the animal's neck and say something soft and soothing in his ear. You'll hurt me because I've let you into my heart.

Oh, God, she'd fallen in love with him.

Tair looked at her paper-pale face and the amusement died from his face. 'You really are scared of horses, aren't you?' He gave a self-recriminatory grimace and, casually looping his leg over the animal's back, he slid down to the ground.

He lifted his hand and raised his voice to a young boy standing a few feet away who immediately came running over. Tair handed him the reins and, shooting a shy smile in Molly's direction, the boy led the animal away.

'I suppose you think that display was smart?' Her chest swelled with indignation as she added in a voice that quavered with emotion, 'I suppose you think that you looked good?' He always looked good. 'Well, just for the record, and because I don't suppose anyone else will tell you because it's probably against the law to tell someone with blue blood they're a posy prat, but it wasn't smart, it was s-stupid and irresponsible and it would serve you right if you were lying on the floor.' She looked at the dusty floor and imagined him there. 'With y-your neck broken, and blood… I can't decide if you're an adrenaline junkie or just a selfish show-off. Either way I…'

She stopped mid-rant just to draw breath and it dawned on her with horror that she had been yelling at the top of her lungs. With a gulp she pressed a hand to her mouth and struggled to hold back the floods of tears that she knew were only a blink away. She waited tensely for Tair to respond in some way to her emotional outburst. Way too emotional… If she didn't keep a tighter control he was going to guess her true feelings for him and that would be too mortifying to bear.

His eyes, concealed behind the mirrored surface of his shades, made it impossible to read what he might be thinking. A nerve clenching and unclenching in his lean cheek as he stood there looking at her was about the only clue—though not much of one. Just when she thought he was not going to react at all he expelled a long sigh.

'I'm an adrenaline junkie,' he confessed.

She blinked as he pulled off the designer shades. The blaze of blue sent any control she'd managed to regain flying out the window.

'When you marry me you can tame me of the habit.'

'I don't want to tame you.' Why would any woman want to change the things that attracted her to a man in the first place?

Which might be a relevant realisation if you were actually going to marry the man, Molly.

'I'm sorry I scared you.'

Now able to read his expression, she was disturbed by it and her eyes fell from his. She shrugged. 'I don't like the sight of blood…any blood,' she added.

'Don't spoil it, Molly. I was feeling so special.'

She lifted her head, prepared to deliver a stinging retort to this mocking comment, only to find he was looking at her with nothing that resembled mockery.

He was looking at her with a kind of…*longing*…and she was so shocked that she said the first thing that popped into her head—which in her experience was nearly always a mistake and this time was no exception.

'You are special.' She glared accusingly at him, then, without intending to, took a step closer.

'You look stunning.'

She made a last-ditch attempt to resist the tug of his eyes. 'I look like I'm auditioning for a place in your harem, but don't get the wrong idea. I didn't dress like this for you.'

'Of course not,' he said, the amused placatory note in his voice bringing a resentful sparkle to her eyes. The resentment morphed to blushing confusion as he added throatily, 'But you'd get the place.'

'I wouldn't take it. I'm not joining the ranks of the thousands of stupid women who would stand on their heads to get your attention.'

'You really do not need to go to such lengths to get my attention, Molly. As my wife your place is assured.'

Struggling to maintain a façade of calm was not easy when her insides were melting and her brain refused to think about anything but his mouth. Eventually she managed to say, 'And I would like to be informed the moment my own clothes are—' She stopped dead as she found herself looking directly into his eyes. There was nothing covert about the message glowing in the azure depths.

Molly was instantly submerged by a wave of longing so strong that for a second her nervous system was totally paralysed.

'I can't take my eyes off you.'

'Oh, God!' she groaned, lifting a shaky hand to her trembling lips. 'Don't say things like that.'

'I thought you liked the truth?'

'So did I.' She lifted her shoulders and gave a distracted little grimace before revealing in a rush of honesty, 'But I don't know anything any more, Tair. I don't even know myself.' The woman she had seen in the mirror with the luminous eyes and secretive smile had not been her—it couldn't be. She didn't fall in love.

Tair could identify with her confusion.

In past relationships it had not been accidental that his partners had never asked where the relationship was going. He did not do emotional soul-searching and he did not get involved with women who were inclined that way.

Tair had never had a sexual relationship with anyone who touched him on an emotional level and vulnerability was not a quality that he had ever sought in a woman.

So why did he respond the way he did to the perplexed pleat in Molly's smooth brow, the little wobble in her voice, and the bewildered look in her wide eyes? It was incomprehensible.

He felt a totally foreign urge to take her tenderly in his arms and find the words to soothe her.

Tair didn't fight the compulsion, but neither did he look too deeply within himself for its source as he stretched out his hand and let his thumb stroke her cheek. These were feelings he had never expected to find within or outside marriage.

The need to soothe became quickly submerged by a much more primitive, more compelling need as he felt the silky smoothness of her warm flesh and was reminded of how she felt beneath him—smooth and soft and hot. The hard kick of desire in his belly was physically painful as he framed her face between his hands.

'You're very beautiful.'

Mesmerised by the glow in his eyes, Molly leaned into him. 'It's the dress,' she whispered past the emotional constriction in her throat. She twitched the jewel-bright fabric with her hand and thought how much she wanted him. 'It isn't beige,' she said. And neither was Tair.

But her life *was* and it would be again, as soon she would be going back to it.

Her spirits took a downward lurch.

She turned her face a little, pressed her lips to his palm and told herself that she didn't really belong here in the desert, or in Tair's bed. There was no question of marriage... that would be insane. But while she was here it would be criminally stupid not to make the most of this little interlude.

An interlude that would always be precious to her, and one that she was definitely going to extract every last shred of pleasure from.

His dark head dipped towards hers and she closed her eyes, anticipating his kiss, feeling a serious anticlimax when his hands fell away from her face.

A moment later he swore.

She opened her eyes and saw he was staring out into the desert presumably seeing something that was way more interesting than kissing her. She resisted the strong impulse to remind him that she was the one he'd been kissing and shaded her eyes to follow the direction of his gaze.

At first Molly couldn't see anything, but then she caught the glint of sun reflecting off metal.

Slowly the silver ribbon in the distance and the cloud of dust above it got closer and defined itself as a convoy of vehicles.

CHAPTER ELEVEN

'YOU have visitors.'

Tair flicked Molly a look and put his hands on her shoulders. 'Yes.'

Molly took a shred of comfort from the contact and the fact he didn't sound any more pleased than she felt. She felt his long fingers tighten on her as the convoy stopped a few hundred yards away.

The sun shone off their tinted windows. At her side she was aware of Tair stiffening, and she glanced at him, a questioning look on her face just as the driver got out of the first vehicle.

Tair just shook his head, took his hands from her shoulders and said in a flat voice, 'Go inside, Molly.'

She ignored him.

'I said, go inside, Molly,' he repeated, his eyes trained on the driver scurrying around to open the passenger door.

'I heard you. I'm ignoring you.' Was her presence an embarrassment to him? The possibility hurt more than it should have.

'Please, Molly.'

'That was nicer,' she approved, still determinedly standing where she was.

She had read somewhere, and it had seemed sensible at the

time, that you should establish some ground rules at the beginning of any relationship.

But this wasn't the start of a relationship or anything else. Molly turned her head as without warning her eyes filled with tears. It was one thing to acknowledge something on an intellectual level, but to be forced to do so emotionally was not nearly so easy to deal with.

At least he didn't know she loved him, though, strangely, the recognition of how much worse things could be did not make her feel better.

'Fine, Molly, message received, you don't do orders. But I really don't have time for this, so just do as you're told for once without an argument...'

He sounded so weary that she struggled to respond with the necessary level of belligerence the comment justified. The lines of strain bracketing his mouth worried her, which was stupid because if ever a man knew how to look after himself it was Tair.

'Have you any idea how sexist that sounds?'

He flashed her a look that said he didn't care, which about summed up his attitude to political correctness, but before she could respond to this silent provocation the driver, who had been joined by four tough-looking individuals clad in traditional white desert garb opened the passenger door and bowed his head.

Molly heard Tair swear softly under his breath as a man dressed in a similar fashion to the others emerged.

There the similarity ended.

Molly didn't need to see the other men bowing respectfully low to tell her this man was in charge; it was written all over him. The same, she realised, was true of Tair. His title was not the reason people showed him respect—he was simply the sort of man that people looked to when there were difficult decisions to be made. Tair was the man who made tough choices and took both the responsibility and the consequences that went with those decisions.

And who did Tair turn to for support? Was that one aspect of being the archetypal alpha male that was hidden away in the small print…?

This new alpha male didn't look as though he found the role a burden. He wasn't young, but it was difficult to gauge his age very precisely because, despite the lines in his leathery dark-skinned face, he stood erect and moved like a youthful man. She could feel the vitality he exuded from where she was standing.

He also exuded anger and towering disapproval.

The four muscular men took up positions at his side, their attitudes alert as they scanned for hidden enemies. The most disturbing factor from Molly's point of view was their sinister accessories, such as the rifles the men wore slung over their shoulders like fashion items. To her relief they showed no sign of pointing them at anyone and instead they bowed very low and respectfully to Tair, who nodded his head in response and said something in his native tongue.

They glanced towards the older man, who nodded almost imperceptibly as if confirming the order that Tair had given. He then walked towards them, before stopping a few feet away.

Tair moved in front of her a little.

It was tempting to tell herself the gesture was protective and that he was trying to shield her from the stern visitor's disapproval, but she knew it was much more likely he was embarrassed by her presence. Maybe this incident had achieved what she had failed to—he had finally realised that she did not fit into his life.

It shouldn't hurt, as she knew that despite his reluctant proposal Tair's feelings towards her went no deeper than sexual attraction, but it did anyway.

It hurt like a dull knife sliding between her ribs into her aching heart.

Pride made Molly lift her chin another defiant degree. She had nothing to be ashamed of. If you discounted stupidity, that was. She was stupid, not because she'd fallen in love, although that wasn't the smartest thing to do, but because she'd previously thought with a mixture of arrogance and ignorance that falling in love was something you had a choice about!

She stepped out of Tair's shadow, leaving her semi-concealment, and with her chin still raised said without looking at him, 'I'm sorry if you're ashamed of me, Tair, but I'm not about to hide away to spare your blushes in front of your friends.'

Tair muttered a savage imprecation and spun her around. One hand in the small of her narrow back, he curved the other around her chin and forced her face up to his.

When she had said blushes Molly had not actually believed him capable of that weakness, but the dark streaks of colour she could see running along the angle of his cheekbones suggested otherwise.

'Ashamed?' he bit out, apparently oblivious to the audience. 'The only thing I am ashamed of is having taken your innocence.'

She could hear the self-recrimination in his voice and in the space of a single heartbeat Molly went from rigid and defensive to melting and unguarded. The depth of her emotions shone in her amber eyes as she lifted a hand to his cheek. 'You didn't take…I gave.'

He inhaled sharply and groaned something in Arabic before drawing her up on her tiptoes and covering her mouth in a kiss that went on and on.

The kiss was both fiercely possessive and exquisitely tender and there were tears of emotion standing in her eyes when he finally lifted his mouth from hers. They stayed close, lips not quite touching, motionless, eyes locked, breaths mingling. Tair's fingers trailed in her hair, his fingertips brushing the sensitive skin on the back of her nape, making her shiver.

It was Tair who broke the tableau. He drew a breath and said, 'Come.'

Molly stared for a moment at the hand extended to her, then reached out and allowed her fingers to be enfolded in his firm warm grip.

It took a few seconds for Molly to fight clear of the sensual thrall that enveloped her, and when she did her glance connected with the dark beady stare of the silent visitor. Her eyes opened wide as she was totally unnerved to realise she had forgotten he was there. She dredged a smile from somewhere and looked to Tair, her expression questioning.

'Molly, this is my grandfather, Sheikh Rashid bin-Rafiq.'

Molly's eyes widened, and she felt a slow flush of intense embarrassment wash over her skin as she became conscious that they had embraced in front of Tair's grandfather.

Great! As first impressions went this one took some beating. Presumably this conservative Arab sheikh, the product of a very different culture from her own, now had her mentally listed under the heading of shameless hussy. Maybe she should enjoy her notoriety and do something really shocking? It was an interesting idea, but her experience of shocking was severely limited.

'Grandfather, this is—'

'I know who she is, Tair.' The dark eyes flicked over Molly before he turned his frowning attention to his grandson. 'It is your identity I am unsure of.' He looked at Tair and shook his head. 'I am most displeased.'

There was a spark of annoyance in Tair's eyes as he gave his grandfather an ironic bow. 'I'm sorry to have incurred your disapproval, Grandfather. I offer no excuses.'

The old man gave a snort. He glanced towards the stationary vehicles and in a lowered voice enquired, 'Have you lost your mind?'

Tair's lips curved into a sardonic smile. 'It is possible.'

The sheikh threw up his hands. 'I am out of patience with you.'

Clearly he was not the only one as almost before the words had left his mouth the door of the second vehicle was suddenly flung open and two men got out, the first in an explosive fashion, the second with a lot more reluctance.

The sheikh turned his head and said in a voice of irritation, 'Tariq, I thought we agreed—'

'I tried to hold him back,' Khalid cut in, huffing a bit as he quickened his pace to keep up with his brother who was striding towards them.

Twenty-four hours earlier Molly would have been ecstatic to see her brothers, but now her emotions were far less clear-cut.

The older man walked to intercept them. 'I thought we agreed you wait until Tair had a chance to tell me what is actually going on.'

'I can see what's going on!' Tariq retorted, slinging Tair a murderous glare. Tair just stood there looking unapologetic.

Molly squeezed her eyes closed. This was a nightmare!

'This isn't what it looks like,' she said, trying to pacify the situation.

Beside her Tair stiffened. 'Yes, it is.'

The quiet provocation drew a sharp hiss of anger from Tariq.

'I was talking to *them*, not you, Tair. And please do not start telling me to go indoors.' She turned to her brothers. 'This is all totally unnecessary.' Her last observation was addressed to all of the men and as far as she could tell made no impression on any of them.

'Let her go!' Tariq gritted, his eyes on Tair's fingers curled around her wrist.

'Tariq, calm down. What are you doing here anyway? I thought Beatrice was ill.'

'She's better.' Her brother's eyes searched her face. 'Are you all right?' The narrow-eyed glance he slid in Tair's direction made it pretty clear where he would lay the blame if she wasn't.

Very aware of Tair beside her, she tried to smile. It was clearly essential to diffuse this potentially explosive situation and as no one else showed any interest at all in playing peace-maker the role seemed to fall to her.

'I'm fine.' It seemed churlish to say that she didn't want to be rescued, so she struggled to adopt an expression approaching welcome as she moved to meet them halfway.

Her brothers stopped about a foot away and for a long moment nobody said a word. The aura of violence shimmering in the air as Tariq and Tair locked glances was almost tangible.

It was Tair who broke the silence.

The next few exchanges were in Arabic, with a few hair-raising French curses thrown in, but it wasn't exactly hard to get the general gist.

Khalid, who had not taken part in the interchange, was staring at Molly. 'Is that really you, Molly?' He shook his head. 'You look incredible.'

'Thanks, Khalid,' she said, then turned to Tair and Tariq. 'Look, you two, all this macho posturing is quite unnecessary. It's all just a silly misunderstanding…it's funny, really.'

Nobody laughed.

'I'm leaving, but not without Molly,' Tariq said.

Khalid cleared his throat and impressed Molly with his bravery by stepping between the two older men. 'Look, let's be sensible about this—nobody wants a fight.'

At that point Tariq landed a solid right to Tair's jaw. Tair, who was driven back several steps by the impetus, made no attempt to avoid it or retaliate. He just stood there looking so noble that Molly wanted to scream. Then she saw the blood and her stomach lurched.

Tariq, who looked disappointed by his cousin's response or, rather, lack of it, was too slow to stop Molly flying to Tair's side.

'Oh, my God, you're bleeding!' she cried in horror. 'Look what you've done, Tariq—how could you?' She sent her brother a fierce glare as she touched the blood seeping from the corner of Tair's mouth with her fingers.

'Come away from him, Molly,' Tariq warned.

Molly gritted her teeth. She was so sick of men and their orders.

'It is fine, Molly. Do not fuss, and it is nothing more than I deserve,' Tair said, appearing totally unappreciative of her frantic mediator act. 'It makes it no better, Tariq, but I did not know when I—'

'Abducted her,' Tariq finished for him.

There was a flush along Tair's cheekbones as he nodded and continued speaking, this time in his own tongue. From her brother's exclamations and the glances in her direction she assumed that Tariq was given a brief explanation.

When Tair stopped speaking Tariq turned to her.

'Why didn't you tell him, Molly?'

It was bad enough having Tair make this her fault, but she wasn't going to take that from her brother.

'Khalid is the one who told him I was Bea's friend to begin with, and you, Tariq, asked me to consider your father's feelings.'

Tariq turned to Tair. 'I still don't see how you could think I would have an affair, Tair?'

Beside his brother, Khalid cleared his throat. 'Before you

get on your high horse, Tariq, you might recall that there was a time when *you* thought *I* was in love with Bea.'

Tair, speaking quietly, interrupted the brotherly interchange. 'She tried to tell me—' Tair's eyes glanced at her face '—and I didn't believe her. I'm sorry, Molly, and I beg your pardon for believing the things I did about your relationship with Tariq. My actions to you were inexcusable.'

'No argument here in that score.' Despite his words, Tariq looked visibly mollified by the unstinting apology.

Sheikh Rashid, who had watched the scene silently, now stepped forward.

'We will discuss this situation in more comfortable and private surroundings.'

It was not an invitation and all the men responded as such.

CHAPTER TWELVE

THE sheikh, who had arranged himself on a pile of silken cushions, impatiently waved away the refreshment and the people who offered it and waited for Molly and the three men to sit down.

Once he was satisfied that he had everyone's undivided attention he spoke. 'Of course you will marry her.'

It was not a question, just a simple statement of fact.

Tair inclined his head in acknowledgement. 'We have discussed it.'

Molly knew that in the future she would always associate the scent of incense that hung heavily in the air with insanity. Not that her future was likely to hold many incense-laden moments, which could not be a bad thing.

So why did her heart sink to somewhere below her knees at the thought of a return to her neatly ordered existence? Would it be that simple? she wondered uneasily. Getting on the plane would obviously be no problem, but would distance put an end to the fragmented steamy images that kept flickering across her vision at the most inappropriate of moments?

And would it stop the empty ache in her heart?

'I think we should settle on a date now.'

Out of respect for Tair's grandfather, Molly compressed her lips, locking the slightly hysterical laugh in her aching throat.

She watched her brothers exchange glances.

Khalid looked as if he wished he were somewhere else, a sentiment that Molly could readily identify with, and Tariq looked only a shade less grim than Tair.

'My uncle might feel awkward about their marriage,' Tariq remarked to nobody in particular. They were all acting as though she weren't there, a circumstance that Molly was finding increasingly aggravating.

The sheikh smiled grimly. 'Leave my son-in-law to me. I have some leverage in that direction.'

Tariq nodded. 'The wedding will therefore take place at the palace as soon as possible.'

Molly stared at the grave faces. This had to be an elaborate joke. Any minute now someone would laugh and shout, Got you!

Molly's eyes moved from one man to the next, her incredulity deepening—nobody was laughing yet. 'Have you all gone mad?'

They finally acknowledged her presence.

Tariq patted her hand in a soothing manner that made her want to scream. 'I understand that it isn't an ideal situation, Molly.'

Molly snatched her hand away and shrieked, 'Ideal!' She gave a hard laugh. 'It's insane is what it is! You lot look sane, but actually you're all stark raving mad! I thought you two at least were civilised,' she said to her brothers. 'Tair does not *want* to marry me.'

The pause before the sheikh spoke was ample time for Tair to say there was nothing more he would like in the world than to marry her. But of course he didn't and stupidly she felt totally bereft.

'It really does not matter what Tair wants,' Tariq explained soberly. 'He knows his duty.'

The sheikh looked sympathetic but his manner was unyielding as he added by way of explanation, 'My grandson has insulted, not just you, Molly, but your family. He will do the right thing, the only thing that is possible in this situation for a man of honour.'

Molly's hands balled into fists. 'I'm not being married off like a piece of damaged goods. People,' she exploded, 'do not get married just because they've had recreational sex!'

For the first time since this conversation had begun Tair's expression of stoic calm slipped and Molly was shocked by the blaze of white-hot anger in his incandescent eyes.

On some level Tair knew his rage was irrational, but that level was deeply buried under layer upon layer of gut-clenching fury. But for some reason hearing her reduce what they had shared to a sordid, shallow level felt like a betrayal, which he knew was ridiculous.

Almost as ridiculous as the fact that last night had been the most intense experience in his life.

'You will not speak in that manner,' he said, glaring at her.

The autocratic decree sent Molly's chin up a belligerent notch. 'I will speak in whatever manner I damned well please,' she growled back. 'And if it wasn't recreational, Tair,' she challenged, 'what was it? True love?' she taunted.

Tariq spoke before Tair responded to her jibe. 'Molly,' he reproached. 'You are being unreasonable.'

Her jaw dropped. Tariq of all people was siding with Tair—talk about male conspiracy.

'How is it everyone else can discuss my sex life but me?' she demanded shrilly.

'I'm sorry, Sheikh,' Tariq said, turning to the older man who had gone rigid at her outburst. 'My sister doesn't understand.'

Eyes blazing, Molly turned on her brother. 'Don't you *dare* apologise for me.' Taking a deep breath, she struggled to regain her control as she turned to Tair's grandfather. 'I'm sorry, Sheikh, but I didn't mean to offend you.'

The sheikh read the genuine remorse in her eyes and nodded his head graciously. 'You appear to be a creature of strong passions, young lady.'

Molly gave another grimace of apology. 'I respect your customs and your beliefs,' she promised. 'I really do, but you have to see they're not mine.'

When he nodded his head she took it as encouragement.

'The thing is the only connection I have with this…' glancing around the exotic and utterly foreign surroundings '…is the fact my mother married a king, couldn't hack it and ran away. Genetically speaking I'm probably the worst woman in the world to marry a prince.'

'Young lady, you are forgetting the fact that your brother will be King of Zarhat and that you are under the cloak of his protection.'

'I don't need protection.' Molly struggled to get her point across even though she sensed she was losing the battle.

'It is not a question of what you need.'

'I'm not royal, I'm an ordinary teacher,' she said, a hint of the desperation she was feeling in her voice. 'I'm like thousands of others. I don't eat off gold plates, I eat microwave meals, I watch soaps, I cycle to work…'

The sheikh looked sympathetic but remained firm. 'My grandson abducted you and stole your innocence. Honour decrees…'

Molly covered her ears with her hands and closed her eyes. She stayed that way until someone took hold of her wrists and brought her hands down.

Even before she opened her eyes she knew it was Tair. 'Go away!' she pleaded. When Tair was near her common sense went out the window. Things flew out of her mouth that were as much of a shock to her as anyone else, and they got her into trouble. Who was to say she wouldn't agree to marry him, just as she'd said yes to making love with him?

She needed to keep in very close contact with her common sense right now because a small part of her, the insanely optimistic part that had read too many romances, thought she could make him love her and wanted to say yes to this crazy proposal.

'Just calm down and listen!'

The request drew a low moan from her throat. 'I've listened long enough. You're all insane!' she cried, her glance encompassing all the men in the room. 'And look at you!' she said to Tair, thinking how she could look at him for ever and it would never be enough.

His air of studied cool was fooling nobody, least of all Molly. The signs of strain in his lean face were obvious.

'When I get married I don't want my bridegroom to look as if he's attending a wake. I don't want to be a man's penance. I want to be his love.' Tears stung her eyes as she sniffed and added bitterly, 'I simply can't believe you're suggesting a shotgun marriage and I'm not even pregnant!'

'Romance is all very well, Molly, but arranged marriages have been working for generations.'

'Like the arranged marriage you have with Bea, I suppose. I have heard a lot about honour, but not a lot about common sense. And, for the record, Tair did not abduct me.'

Tariq's brows meshed. 'What are you talking about, Molly?'

'He said that because he was trying to protect me.'

In the periphery of her vision Molly was conscious of Tair staring at her.

'I asked him to take me with him.'

'No, she didn't.'

Molly flung him a frustrated look. Couldn't he see she was

trying to help him out here? She tried to send him a message with her eyes.

It was a message he either didn't hear or chose to ignore.

'I abducted her.'

The sheikh, looking impatient, waved a bejewelled hand. 'Well, whoever abducted who, the fact is she was an innocent—'

'No, I wasn't.' She felt their eyes on her and lifted her chin. She felt more comfortable with the lie than the subject.

Tair shook his head. 'She was a virgin.'

They all acted as though they were discussing nothing more intimate and private than the price of a barrel of oil.

Molly felt the colour rise up her neck until her face was burning. They didn't have an ounce of sensitivity between the lot of them!

'That's what I told you!' she choked.

The mask slipped and Tair's anger showed through. 'You told me nothing!'

'Would it have made any difference?'

'No.'

Their eyes locked, Molly's chest tightened and her eyes stung as a jumbled mass of contradictory emotions rose inside her as she got to her feet.

'I wasn't living under the protection of the royal family, and Tair didn't seduce me. That was my idea too. So you see there is no crime of honour. Besides, this is academic.' Molly adopted a cool manner that befitted the voice of reason in this room of crazy people.

'You can plan as many weddings as you like, but it doesn't alter the fact that you can't have a wedding without a bride and I'm not marrying anyone.' Her façade fell away as she turned her gaze on Tair and, in a voice that shook with loathing, said, 'Especially you!'

'This is something that *will* happen.'

'There you go again, thinking something will happen just because you say so. Well, maybe that's worked for you before but not with me.

'When I get married it will be to someone who asks me because I'm the most important person in the world to them. Unrealistic, I know,' she added. 'But I'm willing to hold out and if he never comes along—fine, I'll make do with loads of recreational head-banging sex!'

Tair was aware of little but the dull roar in his ears, his hands curled into fists at his sides. The thought of Molly sharing as much as a kiss with anyone but him, let alone the sex she spoke of, put a hot flame under his control.

She continued defiantly. 'I'm not settling for second-best just to appease your warped sense of medieval family honour. I'm sorry if you don't like it, but that's the way it is.'

Outside the light was fading. It was a similar scene to the one she had arrived to the previous evening. Molly could hardly believe how much had happened to her since then. The camp-fires around the encampment had been lit and their smoke mingled with the cold night air. Molly walked towards one, drawn by the glow.

She stood, watching the sparks dance.

A woman sitting close by left the family group she was with and came across to Molly. With a smile she offered her a plate filled with delicious-smelling spicy food.

Molly smiled but shook her head.

They left her alone, as if sensing that she needed the solitude. The incredible hospitality of the desert people was something that she would never forget.

That and other things.

'That was quite an exit.'

She ignored Tair's voice behind her and resisted the temptation to lean back into the solid warmth and strength she could feel inches away. You couldn't cosy up to a man when you'd virtually just said you'd prefer to extract your own wisdom teeth than marry him. Not if you wanted him to believe it.

'The desert is actually rather beautiful.'

'I thought it scared you.'

'It's growing on me. My mother hated it—it scared her.'

'It doesn't scare you?'

No, you do, she thought.

'Marry me, Molly.'

She closed her eyes and shook her head. 'Why?'

'Because, though modern society does not acknowledge it, there is such a thing as the right things and duty and service.'

And love and romance.

'Obviously such an offer is tempting…'

'Some women might think so.' Some women might not consider he was second-best.

'Then marry them.'

'Why are you being so unreasonable?'

She turned suddenly, appeal shining in her eyes as she caught hold of his hands within hers. 'Couldn't we go back to the way we were? I could be your mistress… It was what you wanted.'

An expression of baffled frustration mingled with outrage settled on his face as he looked at her. It might have been amusing under other circumstances.

'You want to be my mistress but not my wife? Is that what you're saying?'

'I suppose I am.'

'You must see that is no longer possible. That I would take a woman who is the sister of the future king to bed but not marry her would not be tolerated.'

She threw up her hands in seething frustration. 'I thought you were the royal rebel who slipped the leash of petty protocol whenever possible? How is it all right to marry someone you don't love but it is not all right to make love to the same person?'

'This is not what it's about.'

'So you're saying if I won't marry you…'

'It is marriage or nothing.'

Tears stood out in her eyes as she stared at him outlined against the desert night sky. 'My God, you and your damned ultimatums, Tair,' she said quietly. 'It has to be nothing.'

Without a word he turned and strode away into the darkness.

CHAPTER THIRTEEN

MOLLY's little flat was in a village about five miles from the school where she taught. The village boasted a small shop-cum-post-office, a pub and a tea shop.

It had escaped the development that had changed many similar areas because of a generous landowner who had inserted a strict covenant when he'd left the park and woodland of his ancestral home to the local community, thus effectively preserving the area.

On a Saturday morning Molly was in the habit of taking a run in the park, but this was the third week she had forgone her run and settled for a walk and cup of tea and a scone in the teashop.

Molly was approaching the tree-lined avenue that led to the wrought-iron park gates, her thoughts very much concerned with the other alterations that she would shortly be forced to make to her lifestyle, when someone tapped her on the shoulder.

'Beatrice!' Molly exclaimed, her eyes opening to their fullest extent as she recognised the glamorous red-headed figure. 'What are you doing here? Is…?' She looked around, half expecting to see her brother, her feelings at the prospect mixed.

'No, don't worry, I'm quite alone—except for Sayed, of course.' As if hearing his name the figure who had been standing half concealed in the shadows stepped out. 'And Amid is parked around the corner.'

'Don't you find it weird? The bodyguard thing?'

'I did,' Beatrice admitted, 'but you get used to it.'

Molly doubted she ever could, but then a few months ago she would have been equally sceptical about the possibility she could fall in love with an Arab prince. She'd lived, learned and suffered.

Molly shut her eyes and tried to block the arguments that had been going around in her head ever since she had read that blue line on the test stick.

Essentially nothing had changed, she reminded herself for the millionth time.

Tair still didn't love her, and this time if she accepted the inevitable offer of self-sacrificial marriage there would be no get-out clause because Molly knew that, unlike her own mother, she could never leave her child to be brought up in another country.

But she was equally sure that Tair was the love of her life—her soul mate—and that she would never find what she had with him with anyone else.

It was not surprising that her internal debate never progressed beyond a bad headache.

She pinned on a belated smile of welcome and felt the start of another headache as she said, 'You look fantastic, Bea.'

It was the truth. As she hugged the glowing princess, whether illusion or not, Molly felt the warmth of the contented glow the new mother projected.

She was not surprised when Beatrice did not return the compliment. Molly knew she looked wretched. Her mirror told her that every time she consulted it.

Some mornings just dragging herself out of bed was an effort. So far her colleagues at work had accepted the story that she had contracted a nasty stomach bug while travelling during the summer break, but she knew the excuse had a shelf-life.

'Motherhood must suit you,' she added. Beatrice made a very good advertisement for the role.

'You didn't see me at the two o'clock, three o'clock and five o'clock feeds. I'm suffering from chronic sleep deprivation.'

'Well, you hide it well. How is the baby?'

Beatrice's beam of contentment went off the scale at the mention of the new arrival. 'He is gorgeous and already shows signs of being a child prodigy, much like his auntie.'

'I wouldn't wish that on anyone.' Being set apart from his or her peers was not something Molly would want for any child of hers. 'Not that I can see any child of yours and Tariq being considered a geek.'

Then, because she didn't want Beatrice to think she was canvassing the sympathy vote—whining was not to her way of thinking an appealing quality—she changed the subject.

'You still haven't said—what are you doing here? And where is your gorgeous baby?'

'I left him with Tariq in London. It's the first time so it feels really strange,' Beatrice admitted. 'But I wanted a little chat with you—alone, Molly.'

Molly's brow furrowed warily. 'Me…?'

'First, how is your father?'

Molly smiled. 'He's fine.'

She had arrived home to find that her father had already had his heart surgery. She had been pleased but puzzled about how things had happened so fast. Did waiting lists vanish overnight?

Her equally mystified sisters, who had met her at the

airport, had also not been able to offer an explanation as to how their dad had leap-frogged his way to the top of the waiting list in such a spectacular fashion.

Some sort of government health initiative, I think someone said, was Rosie's response to Molly's enquiries.

Rosie hadn't been able to remember who this someone was and Sue's response to Molly's questions had been impatient.

'Why the interrogation? Who cares? It worked and Dad's better and that's all that matters. Now he doesn't have all those weeks worrying that every time he feels a twinge it's another attack. And wait until you see the hospital, Molly. It's incredible and the staff are lovely.'

When Molly went to visit her father she realised that her sister had not been exaggerating. The private clinic set in woody grounds was more luxurious than many five-star hotels.

The moment she saw the place she knew what must have happened and it turned out she was right.

The hospital, when taxed, admitted that her father was a private patient, but they had refused to reveal the name of the anonymous person who was footing the bill. Molly, however, had known immediately who it must be.

Now Molly took Beatrice's hand and squeezed it in silent gratitude. 'Thank you to you and Tariq for arranging the private treatment. I'm sure Dad would have been fine anyway, but the waiting and uncertainty was getting unbearable.'

She felt tears of emotion in her eyes that were triggered these days by any little thing, and blinked them back before saying huskily, 'I know that Tariq wanted to be anonymous, but could you let him know how I feel?'

Beatrice looked at her blankly for a moment and then said, 'You think Tariq arranged for your father's operation?'

'Well, didn't he?'

'He would have, if he thought of it, I'm sure, but he had a

lot of other things on his mind around that time, like the baby coming four weeks early.'

Molly shook her head in bewilderment. 'But I don't understand—if it wasn't…then who…?'

Beatrice lifted her brows and the colour rushed to Molly's face as realisation hit like a stone.

'Tair…?' she asked in a small voice.

'Unless you know of any other candidates, I'd say he's a safe bet. Did he know about your dad being ill?'

'Yes.' Molly pressed a hand to her mouth. Bea was right—there was no other alternative. 'This is terrible.'

'Why?'

'I can't be indebted to him like this.'

'Why?'

'Because—' Molly broke off, shaking her head. 'I'll have to say thank you.'

'He won't want thanking.'

Molly felt her anger flare. 'I don't give a damn what he wants! I'm thanking him if I have to tie him down to listen.'

An interesting mental image accompanied this angry declaration, an image distracting enough to make it a full sixty seconds before she realised that Beatrice was staring at her, speculation written all over her face. Molly struggled to compose herself.

'I'm afraid I've had a gut full of bossy men.'

'God, those men!' Beatrice rolled her eyes in comical exasperation. 'When Tariq told me how they'd tried to force you into marrying Tair that way I couldn't believe it!' she exclaimed, shaking her head in disgust.

Molly turned her gaze to the toe of her shoe as though it were the most fascinating thing in the world. 'At least someone knows it would have been a total disaster.'

'I didn't say that.'

Molly's eyes lifted.

'I think you and Tair would make a great couple.' In response to the choking sound that emerged from Molly, the future queen of Zarhat lifted her brows and added with a twinkle in her eyes, 'I mean, there was a frisson between you from the moment you met. Talk about steamy…?'

Molly felt the guilty colour flood her face. 'I didn't… I don't even like him!'

Not like, maybe, but love, adore and feel empty without… Sometimes she felt ashamed of the weakness and her inability to summon up enthusiasm for anything else in life. God, she had turned into one of those people she had always despised!

'I frequently don't like Tariq even now,' Beatrice admitted. 'But I'm always crazy about him.'

'That's different.' Because Tariq loved Bea. Molly felt a surge of envy and was ashamed of it. If anyone deserved to be happy it was Beatrice.

'True,' Beatrice admitted. 'Actually, as things have turned out, you know, you were probably wise. But you already know that.'

I do? Molly gave a noncommittal grunt. 'I think so.'

Although late at night when she couldn't sleep it was sometimes less easy to be sure about her decision, especially since she'd realised that her night of desert passion had not been without consequences—long-lasting consequences.

She would have been tempted to offload the secret she had been unable to share with anyone on Beatrice had she not been concerned the news would filter through to Tariq. Not that Beatrice would deliberately betray a confidence, but Molly knew Bea was totally unable to conceal even the most minor detail from her husband.

There were other people who needed to know before her brother, and it was the reaction of one of those people that was occupying her thoughts to the exclusion of just about everything else at the moment.

Beatrice nodded. 'Some people might think you had a narrow escape…'

Molly's brow furrowed as she knew now that she was missing something. No female who'd met him would call passing on the chance to become the wife of Tair Al Sharif a narrow escape. They might speculate about the mental health of the person who declined, but they wouldn't talk about narrow escape.

'Escape?'

'It sounds hard, but you've got to be practical, even if you are crazy mad in love with someone.' Molly stiffened and then relaxed her guard fractionally as Beatrice added seamlessly, 'Which you're obviously not, but what I'm saying is…' She stopped, clicking her tongue as she disentangled a fallen autumnal leaf from her bright hair, and Molly struggled to contain her impatience.

'Where was I?' Beatrice questioned once her hair was smooth and leaf-free. 'Oh, yes,' she said, picking up her thread just before Molly imploded. 'Even if a person were madly in love they'd think twice before they took on that sort of baggage.'

Molly swallowed her exasperation and wondered if Beatrice could be more vague if she tried. 'What sort of baggage, Bea?'

'Well, Tair's future is not exactly secure with everything that's going on.'

'What?' Apprehension lay like a cold stone in the pit of her stomach. She tried not to think the worst, although for that matter she didn't know what the worst could be.

'You haven't heard, then?' Beatrice asked, looking innocent as she studied Molly's white face.

Molly gritted her teeth. 'Heard what?' She was seriously tempted to shake the information out of Beatrice. It would be worth being rugby-tackled by the bodyguard to be put out of her misery!

'Well, just after you left, Tair's father had a brain haemorrhage. They thought he would die, but he didn't. He's in what they call a persistent vegetative state. He could go tomorrow or stay like that for years, apparently.'

'So what does that mean for Tair?'

'He's King in all but name.'

'But you said it was insecure?'

Beatrice nodded. 'Apparently Tair didn't hang around. He has already made some pretty sweeping reforms and a lot of people who were on the gravy train in his father's time are not happy bunnies. A few of the more influential ones have been stirring it, starting rumours, suggesting that there are better people for the job than Tair.'

Molly's chest swelled with the strength of her indignation. 'But there isn't!'

Beatrice made a soothing gesture in the direction of her bodyguard, who had instinctively stepped forward.

Molly took a deep breath and moderated her tone. 'They couldn't oust him, could they?'

Beatrice gave a careless shrug. 'Who knows?'

Molly had always liked Beatrice, but this callous display of indifference appalled her. 'But he does have people who believe in him and what he's trying to do?'

'Tair does have a lot of support,' Beatrice conceded, 'but he doesn't have an heir, and the cousin that his enemies would like to see on the throne does. An heir and God knows how many spares.'

Molly's thoughts raced. 'So you think that Tair might marry to solidify his position?'

Beatrice shrugged again. 'He's certainly under a lot of pressure to do just that,' she admitted.

Molly gasped as a shaft of jealousy lanced through her with the viciousness of a knife blade. The thought of Tair married to a woman who would give him an heir and the requisite number of spares made her feel physically ill. The level of animosity she felt towards this unknown woman was shocking.

Molly could almost hear the sound of her shredded self-control finally snapping. 'No!' she yelled. 'He can't!' She saw Beatrice's expression and added quickly, 'Nobody should be forced into marriage for political reasons.'

'I know, but Tariq says Tair does have a very strong sense of duty. He thinks he'll put his country before his own happiness. But enough of politics,' she said, taking Molly's arm and adopting a coaxing smile as she led her through the open park gates. 'I came to invite you personally to my party.'

'Party?' Molly echoed, thinking she didn't give a damn about parties right now.

'A birthday party and, before you say a word, I promise there will be no kidnapping this time. Please come, Molly. It's a double celebration—my birthday and you'll be able to meet little Rayhan. He really is gorgeous,' the proud mother declared, her face softening as she spoke of her baby son. 'Please say you will. I know Tariq and Khalid want you to come. They still think you're mad with them.'

'I'm not…'

'I know you're not, but it won't do them any harm to go on thinking that for a little while. They could both do with a dose of humility. So you will come?'

'Will…will Tair be there?' Molly asked casually.

'Not if you don't want him to be.'

'No, I'm fine. Don't exclude him because of me.'

'Well, I have to say, Molly, I really admire your attitude.'

Molly, conscious of her ulterior motives, gave a slightly guilty shrug. 'Well, we're all grown-ups, after all.'

Beatrice laughed. 'I hope you're excluding the men from that statement. Now, come on, I need a cup of tea and I saw a sweet little teashop when we were driving into the village.'

CHAPTER FOURTEEN

'I MIGHT,' Molly conceded as she viewed herself in the full-length mirror, 'have put on a few pounds since I bought this dress.'

'In all the right places,' Khalid inserted with a mock leer as he avoided the blow his pretty blond wife Emma aimed at his ear.

Molly joined in the laughter, but she cast a last worried look at her reflection before she joined the other members of her extended family.

The retro-fifties look of the ballerina-length full skirt with its layers of frothy petticoat had appealed to her the moment she'd tried it on and at the time the lightly boned bodice of her strapless creation had seemed relatively modest.

That was before she had moved from a modest B to an in-your-face C cup seemingly overnight.

The others left the room and Molly lingered, doubting her ability to face the throngs of people that waited in the ballroom below.

'You look like a pole dancer,' she told her reflection before she took a deep breath and responded to the distant appeal from Khalid to get a move on.

As she walked into the room Molly's breath caught in her

throat. Architecturally, the room, a vast hall with its mosaic floor and vaulted ceiling inlaid with gold and lapis, was always magnificent. But the interior decorators had gone to town for the party and the place literally sparkled. Not just with the banks of snow-white sweet-smelling lilies and the glittering décor, but the people, especially the women, were equally dazzling.

The collection of scintillating jewels around the ladies' necks must be giving the security firm nightmares, Molly thought. They were certainly giving her confidence a severe battering.

People turned as they entered and, even though she knew they were not looking at her but the royal couples and the birthday girl in particular, Molly froze like a rabbit caught in the glare of headlights.

Then she heard Beatrice say in a sarcastic undertone to her husband, 'I love your unique take on a few close friends, darling,' and she relaxed a fraction. She felt better to realise that even the ultra-confident and elegant princess found walking into this daunting.

Tariq gave a shrug and admitted that things had got a little out of hand.

'*A little…?*' Beatrice snapped through a fixed smile.

'Later we will have a little party all of our own.'

'Our son might have other plans,' Beatrice retorted before she turned to Molly. 'Look, Molly, I've got to do the hostess stuff but Jean Paul will look after you, won't you, Jean?'

A young man that Molly had not noticed stepped forward. He gave a little bow and smiled. 'I'd be honoured.'

Beatrice and the family group moved away and Molly was left with the Frenchman. Clinging to her sense of purpose and hoping it would pass for poise, she lifted her chin and said, 'You're French.'

'I am, and you are English?'

Molly nodded.

'A real English rose. Would you like to dance?'

'Not really,' she said, her eyes scanning the crowd for one particular face. 'But if you do, I don't mind.'

Her companion looked amused. 'Would I be right in thinking that you do want to dance but not with me?'

Molly's eyes flew back to him, her expression contrite. 'I'm sorry, that was so rude… It's just I'm not very good at all this.'

'Don't worry, my manners are impeccable and I'm a diplomat, my father was a diplomat, my grandfather was a diplomat, so I am very, very good at all this.'

'And modest.'

He gave a rueful sigh. 'Alas, no, the modesty gene was never prominent in our family.'

Molly smiled and held out her hand. 'Shall we start again? I'm Molly.'

'Hello, Molly, I am Jean Paul.' Instead of shaking her hand he bowed low and brushed it lightly with his lips in a courtly fashion, though the expression in his eyes as he lifted his head was not so courtly. He straightened up with her hand still in his.

'Yes, you are very good at this.' He clearly expected her to be charmed and Molly, kind at heart, tried to oblige, but it wasn't easy. The man had the depth of a puddle. Slick and smooth really weren't her thing.

Two months earlier she hadn't known she had 'a thing', but now she knew it was blue eyes, a personality with more twists than a maze, a cruel tongue and a sinfully sensual mouth.

'But underneath the beautiful manners I am a dangerous man.'

Molly, who had met a dangerous man, tried hard not to laugh at the extravagant claim.

'Or at least I try to be—but do not worry. Tonight I am

under strict orders from the lovely princess to behave. I got the impression you are looking for someone…?'

Molly didn't deny it. 'There is someone I need to speak with.'

'And that someone is male…pity,' the smooth Frenchman murmured with a soulful sigh when she didn't correct him. 'Perhaps I could help. I know everyone.'

Molly shook her head. 'It's not important,' she lied.

'Well, until you find who you are looking for, maybe you will allow me to entertain you.'

Molly shrugged. 'Why not?' she said, laying her hand on the arm that was offered to her and not protesting when a hand snaked around her waist.

'So how are you going to entertain me, Jean Paul?' She moved the hand that slipped to her bottom upwards and said firmly but without venom, 'Not like that.'

He gave a philosophical shrug. 'Oh, I don't just know everyone, I know their secrets too. '

Not mine, I hope, Molly thought, smiling. She could see that given time this young man's brand of brittle charm could wear pretty thin.

'I could tell you stories—'

'You mean you're a gossip.'

'I mean,' he corrected, looking unoffended by the accusation, 'that as a diplomat who wants to avoid putting his foot in it and causing offence it pays to know who is getting into bed with who. For instance,' he said, pointing towards a dark-haired beauty in a dress that, though modestly cut, revealed the voluptuous ripe curves of her body, 'not many people know it but that lady is destined to shortly become the wife of a very important man. One of the most important men in the region.'

'Really?' Molly said, pretending an interest. What was she going to do if Tair didn't come?

What was she going to do if he did?

The truth was Molly didn't have the faintest idea what she wanted to happen. Well, she did, but that was not an option because it required Tair to love her.

Every time she played the scene in her head it came out differently. It was, she kept telling herself, too pointless an exercise to speculate this way, but of course she continued to do so anyway.

The only thing left to do now was wing it. Play it by ear.

'So as the wife of Tair Al Sharif she will be a woman to stay on the right side of.'

Molly came to a dead halt, the blood draining from her face as his words penetrated her private dialogue. 'What did you say?'

'I said she—'

Molly interrupted. 'She's engaged to Tair?' Her eyes flew across the room to where the woman in question was holding court to a group of men who looked fascinated by every word she was saying.

She hadn't noticed when Jean Paul had originally pointed the brunette out, but Molly could now see that there was an unattractive hardness about her mouth.

The men around her did not appear too repelled by this deficiency and Molly knew she was searching for flaws in what was by anyone's standard a woman pretty close to perfection. Well, she was only human!

'Not officially, but according to my sources it's only a matter of time. You know the Crown prince, Molly?'

Molly saw the speculation in the Frenchman's eyes and produced a casual shrug from somewhere. 'We have met.'

'Not exactly an easy man, is he?'

Molly, who had called Tair a lot worse to his face, felt her hackles rise at the faintest hint of implied criticism in this observation. 'I think he takes his responsibilities very seriously.'

'Yes, well, he's certainly shook a lot of people up.'

Including me.

'Good evening, Molly.'

The breath left her lungs in one noisy gasp as she spun around, her skirts flaring around her legs like candyfloss.

'Tair…' She hadn't been prepared for what it would feel like to hear his voice again, but then maybe there were some things that couldn't be prepared for—and he was one of them.

The heat exploded in her belly and her legs began to tremble… Like her brothers, he was wearing full traditional dress and he looked incredible. Tall, lean, dangerous, vital and totally, unbelievably gorgeous… Her breath left her lungs in a series of soft fractured sighs as her eyes greedily drank in the details. There weren't enough superlatives to describe the way he looked.

The Frenchman's poise had been momentarily shaken when he'd seen the object of his speculation standing feet away, but he recovered quickly, producing his hand and a brilliant smile. 'Prince Tair.'

Tair, at his most regal or, as Molly privately phrased it, at his most incredibly rude, turned his head sharply, ignoring both the younger man's friendly overtures and the hand extended to him.

Molly found herself staring deep into his blazing blue un-blinking stare, which did not improve her ability to think past the primitive impulse to throw herself at him.

Tair continued to blank the other man totally and kept his eyes trained on Molly's face with an intensity that was drawing a number of curious glances.

'This is Jean Paul.'

Tair inclined his head briefly towards the Frenchman.

'I know who he is.' His eyes still on Molly, Tair bared his teeth in a dismissive smile. 'If you were trying to make me jealous, Molly, you could have done better than *this*.'

The colour flew to her cheeks. 'I was not trying to make you jealous! My God, you're so arrogant, Tair!'

But would she want him any other way?

Turning a deaf ear to the intrusive question, Molly smiled warmly at Jean Paul and laid a hand on his arm. 'You think everything is about you, Tair. You owe poor Jean Paul an apology.'

She lifted her chin and allowed her narrowed-eyed, defiant glare to rest on Tair's lean dark face.

Jean Paul stammered, 'No…no, not at all, I did not know… know that you were both…'

To Molly's utter horror, instead of refuting the assumption or laughing it off Tair lifted his shoulders in an expressive shrug and observed, 'And now you do know.'

Molly rounded on him, her cheeks hot with mortified colour. 'There isn't anything to know.'

'There is no point being shy about this, *ma belle*. It is obvious.'

'The only thing that is obvious to me is that you are totally insane.' She lifted a finger to her own forehead and tapped it sharply. 'Not to mention thoughtless and…' Molly bit her lip, her eyes sliding briefly in the direction of the stunning brunette.

He elevated a dark brow. 'You were saying…?'

Molly averted her eyes and smiled at Jean Paul, who was visibly struggling to cling to the shreds of his diplomatic cool, and ignored Tair. It wasn't as easy as it sounded when she was aware of him down to the cellular level, but she hoped the rigid back she presented him gave him the right message.

While her own feelings towards Tair's prospective bride were not exactly warm and mushy, she did think the woman deserved a little respect and consideration and Tair was not trying to be even slightly discreet. She was conscious that several conversations nearby had stilled while ears were strained to catch what he was saying.

'Prince Tair and I met briefly at a—'

'He doesn't believe a word you're saying, Molly.'

Molly swung back, her eyes blazing liquid gold. 'Will you shut up, Tair?'

She didn't shout at the top of her lungs, but her outburst did coincide with a general lull in the conversation and consequently her furious command—aided by great acoustics—was heard by the nearest hundred people or so.

Molly closed her eyes and groaned. God, Jean Paul was going to dine out on this story for the next ten years! She was not conscious of having voiced her thoughts out loud until Tair said with total confidence, 'Jean Paul is not going to be saying anything to anyone, are you?'

'What would I say? Nothing to say!' He held up his hands in a pacific gesture.

'I'm going to take Miss James off your hands.'

As if she were a piece of excess baggage!

The Frenchman made no attempt to stop Tair when he placed a firm hand in the small of Molly's back and steered her away, but then, Molly reflected bitterly, no one ever tried to stop him doing anything. If they had maybe he wouldn't be the arrogant, overbearing tyrant he was now!

She looked over her shoulder to where Jean Paul was standing staring after them.

'What possessed you?' she hissed at Tair, who carried on walking, ignoring several people who acknowledged him as they passed. 'I hope you realise that Jean Paul is putting the worst possible interpretation on that performance. The man is a gossip.' Presumably in his current situation Tair needed to take care what people said about him. Although he didn't seem to be going quite the right way about it.

'Tair, people are staring. Will you—?' She stopped, her loose hair tangling in the heavy fabric as Tair dragged her through a heavily brocaded velvet curtain and a pair of carved oak doors behind it.

He closed the heavy doors behind them, cutting off the noise from the party like a switch.

Molly, breathless, blinked as her eyes adjusted to the dimmer light of this small antechamber. She backed up until she felt her shoulder blades touch the carved screen behind her and tried to smooth down her hair with her hands.

'Tair…' She jumped as she heard him turn the lock with a decisive click.

CHAPTER FIFTEEN

MOLLY had wanted a private conversation, but not quite this private.

She pressed a hand to her throat where her fluttering pulse throbbed under the pale blue-veined skin.

Tair took a slow measured step towards her. Her oval face looked porcelain-pale and, in the light cast by the blue lantern overhead, slightly other-worldly. She looked perfect and there was nothing other-worldly about the white-hot hunger that roared like a furnace through his veins.

During the last couple of months duty and service had taken precedence, but it had been her face that had kept him going when things had been difficult, along with the knowledge that once he had sorted the mess that had been dumped in his lap he would be free to express the feelings in his heart. Feelings that Tair had not imagined he was capable of experiencing.

When Beatrice had invited him to the party his first inclination had been to refuse, until she had mentioned that they were hoping that Molly would be able to attend.

Suddenly his calendar had become conveniently accommodating.

'What are you doing?' she asked.

'I'm making sure we are not interrupted.'

'Open that door immediately.'

All she could think was how he smelt so good. The lonely weeks of telling herself that she was fine alone, that things would get better, had already been relegated to the level of childish fantasy.

'Why were you so rude to that poor man?'

'Was I rude? I'll apologise to the man some time if that will make you happy,' Tair offered generously. 'I missed you, Molly.'

The husky confession wiped all thought of his appalling manners from Molly's head.

'Did you miss me? Yes, you did, of course you did, and don't try and tell me otherwise,' he warned.

'I wasn't going to,' she admitted.

'I seduced you.'

Molly felt a surge of exasperation. 'You did not seduce me…well, you did, but only because I wanted to be seduced, and it was lovely.'

'Lovely…' He rolled the word on his tongue and nodded. 'Yes, it was, and you are…very lovely. But I wasn't going to apologise, Molly.'

'You weren't?'

He shook his dark head. 'I was going to say that I'm glad I seduced you.'

'Don't look at me like that,' she begged in a small voice.

He shrugged and took another step towards her. 'I like looking at you.' His eyes narrowed. 'Jean Paul is harmless but his hands were all over you.' His eyes slid down her body and his shoulders lifted as he took a deep breath. There was a self-mocking gleam in his eyes as he admitted, 'I did not like it.'

And would he like it when she told him?

Molly's own reaction had been total shock when, on that

morning four weeks earlier, the blue line had appeared on the test paper.

Would Tair be equally stunned? Would he be angry, sad or as ecstatic as she had been after the initial numbness had worn off?

Tair was breathing hard.

'You look beautiful. I would not trust any man with you, even the Jean Paul Duponts of the world.'

The excitement swirling in her veins and the heat in his eyes conspired to make her reckless.

'Does any man include you?' she whispered, barely able to get the words out.

'Especially me, but you already know that.'

Molly tried to focus, but it was incredibly hard when he was looking at her that way. 'I don't know anything. I wasn't sure you'd be here tonight.'

'I wasn't going to be until Beatrice told me you would be.'

Molly's eyes widened as they searched his face. 'You wanted to see me?' It seemed a strange thing to say for someone who was about to marry another woman. Had Jean Paul got his facts right?

Don't go assuming anything…wait to get your facts straight, she cautioned herself.

Facts straight! As if she were capable of cool, objective thought this close to Tair.

'I wanted…' He stopped, his eyes falling from hers as he said something that sounded angry in his mother tongue. 'We parted…' He gave an impatient wave of his hand. 'There were things I should have said that I wanted to say… It must seem to you that you walked out of my life and I forgot you. This is not the case, Molly. Things happened that required my—'

'I know. Bea told me about your father. I'm sorry.' She took a deep breath. 'And I know as well what you did for my dad.'

She saw the caution slide into his eyes. 'Your father?'

His air of exaggerated innocence didn't fool her for a second. 'Just let me say thank you. It was a kind thing to do.'

'I have told you before, and my actions must have confirmed it to you, I do not do kind. The hospital care—it was nothing.' He dismissed the gesture with a shrug of his expressive shoulders.

'A pretty expensive nothing.'

Irritation at her persistence moved at the back of his eyes. 'It was something I could do, very little compared to what I wanted to do…'

The flash of searing emotion she saw when their glances locked made her heart stop dead in her chest.

Maybe she was just seeing what she wanted to. He was marrying someone else…but then why was he looking at her that way?

Her lashes flickered downwards. 'You didn't want to marry me, Tair. You thought you should because of some outdated notion of honour.'

'Honour is not outdated.'

'Some people think that marriage is,' she countered.

'Do you?'

'I've not given it a lot of thought,' she lied. 'I'm very grateful, Tair, for what you did for Dad.'

'I do not want your gratitude!' He saw her flinch and thought how he wanted her soul and her body. He wanted her love, not her gratitude.

'There is no need to yell.' It was not his raised voice that disturbed Molly, but the waves of emotion she could feel rolling off him.

But then if he was under the sort of pressure that Bea had suggested she supposed he would be pretty close to the edge.

He gave a snarling sound of frustration and looked at her with what seemed to Molly like utter loathing.

'I think there is every need to yell.'

'Well, don't blame the people at the clinic. They didn't tell me…when Bea said it wasn't Tariq I knew it must be you.' She lifted her chin. 'I'll pay you back, of course…'

'You will pay me back?' he echoed, looking at her mouth.

'It might take a while, of course…'

He pressed a finger to the groove between his dark brows and swore. 'I really can't decide if you try and insult me or if it just comes naturally to you?'

'The trouble with you is…' You don't love me.

'Why hold back now, Molly? You have never shied away from tearing my character to pieces before.'

'I was sorry to hear about your father.'

Tair shrugged and responded with a painful politeness. 'We have never been close,' he admitted. 'The doctors had warned him this could happen if he didn't reform his lifestyle.'

'But like you he doesn't take orders.'

A spasm of distaste contorted his features. 'I am nothing like my father.'

'Sorry…I didn't mean… I know you're nothing like your father,' she said with a rush. 'It must have been a difficult time for you, but you look well.' He had actually dropped a number of pounds and the weight loss on his already lean, muscle-packed frame had the effect of highlighting the chiselled angles of his proud face.

'You look…' A visible sigh shuddered through his frame. 'As always…I like looking at you.'

His blazing blue eyes had the same effect on her nervous system as being directly connected with the mains supply.

She lifted a self-conscious hand to the exposed upper slopes of her bosom. 'I hope you don't mind me being here.'

'This is your family. I am the guest here.'

'Tair…'

'I like the way you say my name…say it again.'

Molly stared transfixed and whispered softly, 'Tair.' Then she blinked and added brightly, 'I hear you might be getting married.'

He froze and studied her face.

'It is not out of the question,' he agreed.

Everything inside Molly just shut down, including her defences. She struggled to smile but only half got there before disintegrating inside.

'But it is not official yet.'

'It might never be if she saw you drag me out here like that. All I can say is it's not the way I would expect the man I was going to marry to act.'

He angled a dark brow and looked at her miserable face, suddenly appearing more relaxed than he had done since they'd walked into the room. 'And how would you expect the man you were going to marry to act, Molly?'

'I'm not going to marry anyone.'

'You might find someone when you least expect it. That does happen, so I believe…'

'Is that what happened to you? No…don't tell me,' she begged, covering her mouth with her trembling hand. 'I don't really want to know. But I'm very happy for you,' she lied. Being noble and selfless hurt like hell, and Molly could feel her more ignoble jealous self fighting to slip the leash. 'I saw her…Jean Paul pointed her out. She is very beautiful.' The sort who would run to fat in later years.

His lips thinned in distaste. 'Zara is not really to my taste—she is a little too obvious.' And she is not you.

'Then why are you marrying her?'

'I'm not.'

'But, Jean Paul said—'

'So of course it must be right,' he cut in sardonically.

She took a deep breath. 'Of course not…right, well, excellent.'

'Yes.'

'Right, well, excellent.'

'You said that.'

Molly felt something snap inside her. 'Well, I've been out
of my mind with worry since Beatrice told me.'

'Since Beatrice told you what?'

'That you were perhaps in danger.'

He blinked. 'Really? I thought it was just my sanity I stood
in danger of losing.'

'This isn't a joke, Tair!' she yelled, frustrated by his
careless attitude. 'You've never taken security seriously and
now…have you considered wearing body armour?'

Tair looked into her pale, earnest face for a long moment
before asking, 'Just what has Beatrice been saying to you,
Molly? Come sit down here.'

She shook her head. 'I don't want to sit down.'

'Why do you think I need…body armour?'

'Well, Beatrice didn't come right out and say that you were
in *physical* danger, but it follows that these people are dangerous and they're playing for big stakes and they want you
out of the picture any way they can.'

'You are talking about my critics in Zabrania?'

She nodded. 'Beatrice said they want to put a cousin of
yours on the throne. That he has an heir and a spare and…I
suppose that's why you're thinking of marriage…?'

'*Heirs* are the last thing on my mind at this precise
moment, Molly,' he told her honestly.

'That's a pity, because the thing is, Tair…'

'The thing is?' he prompted.

She sucked in a deep breath and lifted her chin. This was
never going to be easy. 'The thing is you've got one, or you

will have in about seven months. I know this is shocking! Are you all right?' She angled a worried look at him.

He looked at her blankly. 'You're pregnant?' His hand fell away. 'Baby…?' His eyes fell to her stomach, then slowly rose to her face.

Molly was shocked by the grey tinge to his skin.

Tair was a man who rolled with the blows and came back for more. His resilience was an integral part of him. But the man standing there staring at her had the look of a man who had just received a mortal wound.

'*Dieu!*' he breathed, dragging a hand across his jaw. 'You are pregnant with our child?'

'I'm sorry.'

Tair blinked to banish the image of her holding a child in her arms from his head.

'Sorry…sorry?' His voice rose to an incredulous boom as he regarded her unhappy face with stark incredulity. '*You're* sorry? I am the one that put you in this position and left you *alone…*' His voice trailed off.

Molly had gone through the stunned stage herself and had some understanding of how he was feeling. 'It does take a while to sink in.'

His searching eyes moved over her before he asked thickly, 'You are well?'

'Fine,' she said, thinking that he didn't look it. 'I want this baby, Tair.'

'*Our baby…*' he said, still sounding as if the news had not quite fully registered.

'I know it might be difficult for you to think about it logically right now, but although you might not be happy about it—'

'Did I say I'm not happy?'

'You didn't have to.'

'I suppose I don't have to say anything either because you

will put words in my mouth. I am going to be a father…' He passed a hand across his eyes and shook his head.

'A baby needs a father.'

His fierce eyes flew to her face. 'Do you think I do not know this?'

'Let me finish, *please*, Tair,' she begged. 'A baby needs a father and your position might be more secure if you were married.'

Something moved behind his eyes. 'Molly, are you proposing to me?'

The colour rushed to her face, but she held his gaze. 'No…yes…I suppose I am,' she admitted. 'The things you said about arranged marriages, you know, actually make sense when you stop to think about it.'

She sounded as if she were selling double glazing!

'No, it doesn't.'

She felt the mortified colour rush to her face and wanted to die. 'Oh, well, it was just an idea.'

'Yes.'

She shook her head. 'Pardon?'

'I said yes, Molly, I will marry you.'

'This isn't a joke, Tair,' she reproached.

'I'm not joking. I've never been more serious in my life.'

'But you just said…'

'I just said that arranged marriages do not make sense. But you were not proposing an arranged marriage, were you, Molly? You love me.'

She held his steady gaze for a moment, then said with defiance, 'Yes, I do.'

Tair's shoulders slumped as weeks of tension fell from them.

His visible relief and the blaze of triumph in his blue eyes were lost to Molly who began to weep, tears sliding down her face.

The sound of her deep sobs made something twist in Tair's chest. 'My dear, fierce, beautiful Molly,' he said, pulling her into his arms. 'Is it so bad loving me?'

She lifted her tear-stained face from his chest, bit her trembling lip and wailed tragically, 'It's awful!'

Unable to resist any longer, Tair bent his head and kissed her hard. 'Is that a little less awful?'

Molly gulped and nodded. 'A bit,' she conceded. 'I'm a bit emotional right now…hormones and…'

His fingers tightened in her hair, pulling her head back so that he could look into her face. 'And you were afraid for me?'

No wonder he sounded so incredulous. He had a team of loyal men willing to lay down their lives for him—and she had acted as though she could make a difference.

'Well, I've seen how reckless you are…and…I know they've isolated you and spread rumours.' Molly breathed in the clean, male, marvellous scent of him and thought how she would never let anyone hurt him.

'And you felt it would improve the chances of my continued health if I married you and you gave me babies.'

She turned her face into his neck and snapped, 'Don't laugh at me, Tair.'

'Believe me, I'm not laughing, *ma belle*.'

'Beatrice said…'

A flash of annoyance crossed Tair's lean face as he laid a finger across her lips. 'It seems to me that Beatrice has said far too much. She has caused you so much anguish.'

'I'm glad she told me. I have a right to know—'

'I'm not in danger, Molly.'

Her narrowed eyes lifted to his face. 'Beatrice wouldn't lie.'

'Not directly,' he conceded. 'But she has bent the truth to the point of snapping. I did upset some influential people when I took control.' He smiled down into her anxious face.

'And they would, I do not doubt, have been more than happy if I vanished, but they have never been in a position to make that happen.'

Molly felt a flicker of cautious relief. 'They haven't?'

'They are in a minority and over the years when they milked the system they made many enemies, some powerful. Those enemies are now my allies. My critics have no popular support among either the people or the ruling classes.'

'So you're not in danger?' she sniffed, still not totally convinced.

'No. The only threat to my authority, the only person who has ever rebelled against me, is you, Miss Mouse.'

The relief now was so intense that Molly felt dizzy with it. 'Oh, God, I've been so *so* worried.' She could smile about it now that he was safe. 'But why would Beatrice say those things if…?'

His lips stretched in a sardonic smile. 'I think Beatrice might have been trying to play cupid.'

Molly began to shake her head in automatic dismissal of such a ludicrous theory and then stopped, a look of shocked comprehension crossing her face. 'My God, she was, you're right, and I didn't tell her about the baby so she's going to think it worked.'

Tair muttered something under his breath and grabbed her by the shoulders, turning her to face him. 'Can you still think that I'm marrying you because of the baby?' he asked incredulously. 'Not even you are that stupid!'

'I'm not stupid…' Her heartbeat quickened as she read the extraordinary message in his eyes. 'But you…can't *want* to marry me.'

He kissed her hard. 'Do not put words in my mouth. I am quite capable of speaking for myself. Thinking about marrying you, Molly, is the only thing that has kept me going during the past weeks.' He reached out to touch a finger to the single tear that had escaped her overflowing eyes and admitted, 'That you are pregnant with our child is admittedly a plus point.'

'You're *glad* about the baby?'

He looked insulted that she could think otherwise. 'I am over the moon about this baby!' He curved a big hand over her stomach. 'And I want this baby because it is ours…yours and mine…and we made it with our love, and I want to marry you because my life is empty without you in it. I love you, Molly Mouse. I love your golden eyes, I love your sharp tongue…I love the entire beautiful, irresistible package. *Dieu!*' he groaned, gathering her in his arms. 'I have been half a man without you these weeks.'

The tenderness in his long, lingering kiss brought more tears to Molly's eyes.

'I can't believe this is happening. I have loved you almost from the first, Tair.'

'Yet when I asked you to marry me you refused me because I was second-best, and that hurt.' The mocking gleam in his eyes was directed at his own stupid pride.

'I refused, Tair, because I didn't want you to marry me out of duty.'

'I know,' he said, taking her small hand in both of his and lifting it to his lips. A delicious shudder rippled through Molly's body as he turned it and kissed her palm.

'I wanted you to marry me out of love,' she said in a throaty whisper.

'And I was too stubborn to admit even to myself that I was in love…' Transferring his attention to the blue-veined inner aspect of her delicate wrist, he continued. 'You have no idea how often I have regretted it in the weeks since.'

'Not as often as I've regretted refusing to be your wife,' she retorted. 'I have been so lonely without you.'

'Good!'

'That is not a very nice thing to say,' she reproached.

'I have told you, Molly, I am not a very nice man.'

'You are the only man I want.'

Heat flared like blue flames in his eyes. 'Or have ever had… You have no idea what it did to me to know that I was your first lover.' His eyes darkened at the memory. 'I should have regretted it but I didn't,' he admitted huskily.

'Neither did I.'

'Tariq is one of my closest friends, but when I thought of him with you I…' Tair shook his head, still shocked by the memory of his primitive reaction.

Molly ran a loving finger down the curve of his cheek. 'I wasn't too happy to see them either,' she murmured. 'I wanted you to myself and I wanted a chance to tell you that I was actually the sister nobody really wanted to acknowledge.' She had understood the situation, but it had hurt.

Tair bent his head to hers. 'Their loss!' he said fiercely as he pulled her into his arms.

With a sigh Molly looped her arms around his neck as he swept her off her feet and kissed her with a ruthless hunger she could feel in her bones.

They were still kissing when there was a loud knock on the door.

'Ignore it,' Tair said thickly.

It was advice that Molly was only too happy to go along with.

The second and third knock she could ignore, but it was more difficult when Khalid's voice called their names through the door. 'Tair… Molly!'

'He knows we're in here, Tair. You have to answer.'

'I don't see why.'

'Because he's not going away.' The bangs were getting louder. 'Tair…?'

He looked at her and heaved a frustrated sigh. 'All right, then.'

Khalid, who seemed oblivious to the lack of warmth in Tair's manner when he unlocked the door, explained that Beatrice needed them in the ballroom. It was an emergency, he explained in response to Molly's concerned questions.

He remained quite vague about what form the emergency took as he led them back into the crowds.

Five minutes later Tair's patience was wearing thin.

He gave a discontented scowl as he looked around the glittering room. 'What emergency? Bea's not here and I don't see why we have to stay.'

Molly gave him a warning glance. 'It would be rude,' she scolded. 'And she wouldn't say there was an emergency if there wasn't.'

Tair bent down, his breath brushing the sensitive skin of her earlobe as he whispered, 'I'm in pain.'

Molly felt a lustful kick in her stomach. 'Behave,' she pleaded without an awful lot of conviction before adding, 'Me too.'

A hush fell over the hall, but Molly, who was still gazing into Tair's eyes, did not notice at first.

'Friends.' The king's voice, aided by excellent acoustics, carried to every corner of the room.

Molly's startled glance flickered to the regal figure who stood in the centre of the hall. She looked at Tair, who shrugged and shook his head.

Molly's attention strayed every few seconds to the man beside her. Her heart was so full of love she felt as though she might explode and she listened with half an ear as the white-haired king wished his daughter-in-law a happy birthday and welcomed his new grandson.

'And lastly,' said the king, 'there is another person I must welcome to our family. My sons' sister, Miss Molly James.'

Molly froze in shock as the crowds opened up between her and the king, a clear corridor down which her brothers began to walk.

It was Tair who pushed her towards them.

Flanked by her smiling brothers, her ears ringing to the sound of clapping hands, Molly walked towards the king. The emotional occlusion in her aching throat thickened as he took her by the shoulders and formally kissed her on both cheeks.

The clapping had begun to die away when she turned and saw Tair walking towards them. His blue eyes held hers as he joined them.

He bowed formally to the king and murmured, 'Honoured, Uncle.' Turning, he took Molly's hand in his before allowing his glance to move over the faces of the avidly curious onlookers.

'What are you doing?' Molly muttered.

'I would like to formally request the hand of Miss Molly James in marriage, Uncle.'

'Is that so, Prince Tair?' The king raised a sardonic brow. 'I have no objections, though I do feel that Molly might do better, nephew.'

'Molly James.' Holding her eyes, Tair dropped down on one knee. 'I have asked you once and you refused me, but I ask you again. Will you do me the great honour of accepting me as your husband?'

Molly, acutely aware of every eye in the room on her and hating the attention, mumbled with a lot less regal confidence than either man, 'Yes, I will.'

Tair grinned in response to her agitated whisper for him to get up and rose with fluid grace before kissing her hand and turning to the room. He announced her with pride that brought tears to her eyes. 'My princess.'

Under the cover of clapping and cheering Molly squeaked, 'If you do that to me again I will never forgive you.'

Tair, looking unrepentant, bent his head to her ear. 'You are mine and I wanted everyone to know it.'

Molly saw the fire of pride and love shining in his eyes and the joy inside her rose up like a warm wave.

She was the luckiest woman on earth!

Without a word she took his face between her hands and kissed him hard on the mouth.

When she released him Tair gave a silent whistle. 'For a woman who doesn't like people staring, Molly Mouse… that was…?'

Molly grinned. 'I want everyone to know you're mine too, Prince Tair.'

'I think,' Tair said, his solemn expression belied by the warmth and laughter dancing in his eyes, 'that someone in the corner over there might not have got the message.'

'In that case…' Laughing, she allowed herself to be swept up into an embrace that left nobody in the room in any doubt about who belonged to whom.

They belonged to each other.

* * * * *

*Harlequin is 60 years old,
and Harlequin Blaze is celebrating!
After all, a lot can happen in 60 years,
or 60 minutes…or 60 seconds!
Find out what's going down in Blaze's
heart-stopping new mini-series,
FROM 0 TO 60!
Getting from "Hello" to "How was it?"
can happen fast….*

*Here's a sneak peek of the first book,
A LONG HARD RIDE
by Alison Kent
Available March 2009*

"Is THAT FOR ME?" Trey asked.

Cardin Worth cocked her head to the side and considered how much better the day already seemed. "Good morning to you, too."

When she didn't hold out the second cup of coffee for him to take, he came closer. She sipped from her heavy white mug, hiding her grin and her giddy rush of nerves behind it.

But when he stopped in front of her, she made the mistake of lowering her gaze from his face to the exposed strip of his chest. It was either give him his cup of coffee or bury her nose against him and breathe in. She remembered so clearly how he smelled. How he tasted.

She gave him his coffee.

After taking a quick gulp, he smiled and said, "Good morning, Cardin. I hope the floor wasn't too hard for you."

The hardness of the floor hadn't been the problem. She shook her head. "Are you kidding? I slept like a baby, swaddled in my sleeping bag."

"In my sleeping bag, you mean."

If he wanted to get technical, yeah. "Thanks for the loaner. It made sleeping on the floor almost bearable." As had the warmth of his spooned body, she thought, then quickly changed the subject. "I saw you have a loaf of bread and some eggs. Would you like me to cook breakfast?"

He lowered his coffee mug slowly, his gaze as warm as the sun on her shoulders, as the ceramic heating her hands. "I didn't bring you out here to wait on me."

"You didn't bring me out here at all. I volunteered to come."

"To help me get ready for the race. Not to serve me."

"It's just breakfast, Trey. And coffee." Even if last night it had been more. Even if the way he was looking at her made her want to climb back into that sleeping bag. "I work much better when my stomach's not growling. I thought it might be the same for you."

"It is, but I'll cook. You made the coffee."

"That's because I can't work at all without caffeine."

"If I'd known that, I would've put on a pot as soon I got up."

"What time *did* you get up?" Judging by the sun's position, she swore it couldn't be any later than seven now. And, yeah, they'd agreed to start working at six.

"Maybe four?" he guessed, giving her a lazy smile.

"But it was almost two…" She let the sentence dangle, finishing the thought privately. She was quite sure he knew exactly what time they'd finally fallen asleep after he'd made love to her.

The question facing her now was where did this relationship—if you could even call it *that*—go from here?

* * * * *

*Cardin and Trey are about to find out that
great sex is only the beginning....
Don't miss the fireworks!
Get ready for
A LONG HARD RIDE
by Alison Kent
Available March 2009,
wherever Blaze books are sold.*

When passion leads to pregnancy!

PLEASURE, PREGNANCY AND A PROPOSITION
by Heidi Rice

With tall, sexy, gorgeous men like these,
it's easy to get carried away with
the passion of the moment—and end up
unexpectedly, accidentally, shockingly

PREGNANT!

Book #2809

Available March 2009

Don't miss any books in this exciting new
miniseries from Harlequin Presents!

HARLEQUIN *Presents*

EXTRA

THE BILLIONAIRE'S CONVENIENT WIFE

Forced to the altar for a marriage of convenience!

He's superrich, broodingly handsome and needs a bride in name only....

She's innocent yet defiant, and she's about to be promoted from mistress to convenient wife!

Look for all of our exciting books in March:

The Italian's Ruthless Marriage Bargain #45
by KIM LAWRENCE

The Billionaire's Blackmail Bargain #46
by MARGARET MAYO

The Billionaire's Marriage Mission #47
by HELEN BROOKS

Jonas Berkeley's Defiant Wife #48
by AMANDA BROWNING

www.eHarlequin.com   HPE0309

REQUEST YOUR FREE BOOKS!

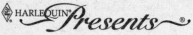

2 FREE NOVELS PLUS 2
FREE GIFTS!

YES! Please send me 2 FREE Harlequin Presents® novels and my 2 FREE gifts (gifts are worth about $10). After receiving them, if I don't wish to receive any more books, I can return the shipping statement marked "cancel". If I don't cancel, I will receive 6 brand-new novels every month and be billed just $4.05 per book in the U.S. or $4.74 per book in Canada, plus 25¢ shipping and handling per book and applicable taxes, if any*. That's a savings of close to 15% off the cover price! I understand that accepting the 2 free books and gifts places me under no obligation to buy anything. I can always return a shipment and cancel at any time. Even if I never buy another book, the two free books and gifts are mine to keep forever.   106 HDN ERRW 306 HDN ERRL

Name _____ (PLEASE PRINT) _____

Address _____ Apt. # _____

City _____ State/Prov. _____ Zip/Postal Code _____

Signature (if under 18, a parent or guardian must sign)

Mail to the **Harlequin Reader Service**:
IN U.S.A.: P.O. Box 1867, Buffalo, NY 14240-1867
IN CANADA: P.O. Box 609, Fort Erie, Ontario L2A 5X3

Not valid to current subscribers of Harlequin Presents books.

Want to try two free books from another line?
Call 1-800-873-8635 or visit www.morefreebooks.com.

* Terms and prices subject to change without notice. N.Y. residents add applicable sales tax. Canadian residents will be charged applicable provincial taxes and GST. Offer not valid in Quebec. This offer is limited to one order per household. All orders subject to approval. Credit or debit balances in a customer's account(s) may be offset by any other outstanding balance owed by or to the customer. Please allow 4 to 6 weeks for delivery. Offer available while quantities last.

Your Privacy: Harlequin Books is committed to protecting your privacy. Our Privacy Policy is available online at www.eHarlequin.com or upon request from the Reader Service. From time to time we make our lists of customers available to reputable third parties who may have a product or service of interest to you. If you would prefer we not share your name and address, please check here. ☐

HP08R

BROUGHT TO YOU BY FANS OF
HARLEQUIN PRESENTS.

We are its editors and authors
and biggest fans—and we'd
love to hear from YOU!

Subscribe today to our online blog at
www.iheartpresents.com

You're invited to join our Tell Harlequin Reader Panel!

By joining our new reader panel you will:

- Receive Harlequin® books—they are FREE and yours to keep with no obligation to purchase anything!
- Participate in fun online surveys
- Exchange opinions and ideas with women just like you
- Have a say in our new book ideas and help us publish the best in women's fiction

In addition, you will have a chance to win great prizes and receive special gifts! See Web site for details. Some conditions apply. Space is limited.

To join, visit us at
www.TellHarlequin.com.